GZ    10/16

ng,
ok!
ken

ESS

# GIRL DETA CHED

# GIRL DETACHED

## MANUELA SALVI

Translated from the Italian
by Denise Muir

First published in 2016 in Great Britain by
The Bucket List, an imprint of Barrington Stoke
18 Walker Street, Edinburgh, EH3 7LP

Text © 2016 Manuela Salvi
Translation @ 2016 Denise Muir

The moral right of Manuela Salvi to be identified as the
author of this work has been asserted in accordance with
the Copyright, Designs and Patents Act, 1988

Excerpt from "Illusion is the first of all pleasures" from
*How to Measure the Sky* © 2012 Dropout-Davide Burattin

Quotes taken from *A Woman of No Importance*,
Oscar Wilde, 1893

A CIP catalogue record for this book is available
from the British Library upon request

ISBN: 978-1-911370-02-4

Printed and bound by CPI Group (UK) Ltd, Croydon, CR0 4YY

*To all the children inside the adults, who know and never forget*

*He touches me, but it's weird because I can feel his hands but he's not beside me, he's over by the door. I see different faces. I can feel my skin against someone else's. They touch me. They adore me. Someone mumbles in my muffled ears, "Never seen anything like it." Or something like that.*

*Then it all goes dark.*

# 1

Helena's banging again today.

I wish she wouldn't. I'd like to tell her to stop, that my head's thumping, that the dust is sticking in my throat, but I can't. The words won't come out, they're stuck inside, throbbing, hurting; so instead I drag my suitcase along and think that one jammed wheel isn't as bad as two. I look at the white line it's making on the faded lino floor, another scratch to add to the collection. It feels like I'm scratching at somebody's soul.

"I-it's c-coming on well," I say when I reach Helena, letting go of my suitcase and catching my breath. She stops hammering and looks at me. I don't like the look in her eyes. They're so full of tension all the time.

"Y-yeah, uh, y-you know, th-the set d-design. It's n-nice," I add, wishing I'd never opened my mouth. I'm starting to stammer too much again. I take a big, deep breath and say *shit, shit, shit* to myself. It works. I feel my tongue relax a bit, and the pain in my chest eases off.

I watch as she picks up a sheet of sandpaper and starts rubbing angrily at the wood. I'd like to be her right now.

I'd like to be anyone else but me, because today I've got no choice but to keep moving, when all I really want to do is scream.

A shower of raindrops suddenly hits me. Cold water drips down the back of my neck and along my spine. But my hair is so bushy that most of the water just runs off and drips onto the floor and my shoes.

"Oops," says a voice from somewhere above me. "*So* sorry, I was trying out the rain effect."

I look up at the ceiling and see our very own Hunchback of Notre-Dame clambering around the rafters and lights. Jonah. He likes to think he's the lights, sound and special effects engineer, but I think the only reason he's here is because he's got nowhere else to go. I'd like to tell him how stupid he is. I'd like to tell him to stop playing stupid pranks. But I don't. I take a deep breath, wipe my face and say, "Ap-p-parently it w-works." I'd never want to be *him*, and that makes me feel a bit better.

I shove my suitcase into a corner behind the scenery and step out onto the stage.

Thomas is there already, along with the other actors, and he's explaining about the rehearsals. He stages shows in a town where no one cares about theatre, using actors who would be good for nothing in the real world. That's us. The homeless stutterer. The hunchback. The mute set designer who never says a word to anyone. And all the other freaks.

Thomas makes fun of us sometimes. "We're a real Ship

2

of Fools," he says. "But there's worse than us out there."

*Ship of Fools*. I don't like the name of the theatre company. I know that centuries ago lunatics would be forced on board ships and cast adrift. That's how they got rid of them. I can't help thinking about those poor people, left to starve or die of thirst, thrown overboard and eaten by sharks, burned up in the sun or shredded to pieces in a storm.

I don't want to be aboard the Ship of Fools.

But I am, because I like acting. My gran wanted me to act. And if I don't act, there's not much else I can do, apart from think, which is what I'd really rather not do, especially today. Especially after the events of the past few days.

"Hey, Alek," Thomas says when he sees me. "You look kind of wet. Is it raining?"

I nod, silent.

He takes a towel from the back of a chair and throws it at me. "Go on, it's your turn. We're all ready."

I'm playing Hester in the play we're rehearsing.

Hester the nice girl. Hester the puritan. Young Hester, who judges everyone else so harshly, but who knows so little about life and the ways of the world herself. When she falls in love, she's willing to change the way she thinks.

I close my eyes and the stage disappears.

I hold my breath. I imagine Hester and her long, swishy dress, the corset holding her upright, the silk shoes, her gloved hands. I straighten my back and I'm no

3

longer wearing a checked flannel shirt, buttoned up and two sizes too big.

I'm not Aleksandra any more.

I'm Hester and I'm at an upper-class dinner party.

Lady Caroline asks me, "Have you any country? What we should call country?"

Smiling, I lift my chin. "We have the largest country in the world, Lady Caroline."

I love Oscar Wilde. The night my gran died, I started learning the lines of the play off by heart, in a panic, sobbing and laughing at the same time. Oscar Wilde knew that life is both pleasure and pain, always mixed up, never just one or the other, always entwined.

Then I choke on one of my lines. Thomas looks up sharply from his script – I never stammer when I'm acting. He raises an eyebrow and I try again.

"Nothing should be out of the reach of hope. L-life is a h-ho-ope."

Thomas signals to the other actors to ignore me and keep going.

And so I wait for the actor playing Gerald – my onstage suitor – to ask me to go for a stroll. I accept and exit the scene with him, advancing into the semi-darkness backstage. I'm Aleksandra again, the 'k' in the middle the only thing I inherited from my dad.

Jonah comes down from the rafters and starts messing about with the lights panel. In a costume drama, set in the 1890s, there's not much to play with, apart from maybe a candlelight effect. All the same, he seems to be taking it very seriously, but that's only because he takes himself so seriously.

"What's with the suitcase?" he asks me out of the blue, while keeping his eyes on his lights panel. "Going on holiday, are we?"

"S-sort of," I reply.

I don't want to talk about it with him. I haven't told anyone, except for Thomas. Putting it into words would make it feel too real. Words are heavy. When you pronounce them, when you're acting, you feel the weight of them. If you mix them up, or get them wrong – say marvellous instead of magnificent, for instance – they sound like nails on a chalkboard. Screeching, raking. In the theatre, Thomas can shout, "No! Do it again!" But it doesn't work like that in real life. If you get a word wrong, if you go off-script, you can't retake the scene. Jonah doesn't seem to understand this. In fact, he's still prattling on in that droning voice of his.

"So, where are you going?" he asks. His long blond hair has slipped out of his bandana. "That case looks way too heavy for a weekend break. There's something serious about it, like it's about to explode. Are we going to be buried under a mountain of lumberjack shirts, Lady Hester?"

He smirks. I think how it's a nice smile, but shifty too. I shrug and concentrate on the scene being played out on stage. I have to go back on very soon.

"Hey, Helena's our resident mute," he says. "How about you s-s-say s-s-something?"

My onstage suitor comes rushing back from the toilet,

hooks his arm in mine and we go back on just in time, Jonah's sniggers still ringing in my ears.

A few lines later, Mrs Allonby – another guest at the party – starts telling me about London dinner parties.

"I adore them," she says. "The clever people never listen, and the stupid people never talk."

"I think the stupid people talk a great deal," I say, throwing an eloquent glance backstage.

"Too strong, Alek. Watch your tone. You're not angry here," Thomas says.

A glaring spotlight suddenly switches on above us and the thousand-watt light shines straight down on me. It feels like I'm in the gravitational ray of an alien spaceship, about to be sucked up into the sky. I have to squint to stop the light from blinding me.

"Jonah." Thomas sighs. "Pack it in."

The light goes off and semi-darkness returns.

"Sorry. Must've been an electrical fault," he says, and although I can't see him snigger, I can hear it.

We're about to pick up where we'd left off, but there's no peace for anyone today. The silence is broken by Helena's hammering – she's started banging again. Her hammering is harder than usual, which means she's not happy about something and is interrupting our rehearsals on purpose. It's amazing how much she can say with just a hammer and something to hit.

"I don't believe it!" Thomas says. I guess that story about the fools cast adrift doesn't seem quite so poetic at times like these. "Helena!" he cries, hands on hips, as if that pose might be enough to intimidate someone who's looking at you like a malevolent raven, waiting for the right time to gouge your eyes out.

Helena comes over, dragging her feet. Her combat boots kick up the dust of the stage, dislodging it from the old, worn wooden planks. Whenever she comes on for anything to do with the scenery, we all wonder why she doesn't act. Her presence lights up the stage, transfixing everyone with the very sight of her, as if we're all holding our breath, waiting for her to say something, anything, even an insult.

She's not one of those girls who only look good with make-up on, in certain clothes, or from a certain angle. She looks amazing just the way she is now, in a pair of baggy denim dungarees, combat boots and a ripped, faded black T-shirt. The dingy rags hanging from her skinny, tense frame contrast with the intense colour of her eyes, making them seem greener than ever.

*What's up?* she asks Thomas by running a hand through her short black hair. Her fingers leave a dusty streak of sawdust behind.

"You're doing an excellent job, but we need to rehearse," he explains patiently. "Can you come back tomorrow after school?"

She looks at him expectantly, like she's waiting for him to say something more, then turns on her heel and leaves the stage. We hear the *clang-clang* of her tools as she gathers them up, then thrusts them into her tool belt. Heavy footsteps follow, the door creaks for a second then bangs shut.

"Maybe you should tell the others," says Lady Caroline, who's actually Thomas's real-life partner, Electra. She's chirpy and plump and playing the part of a 19th-century upper-class Englishwoman suits her.

"Tell us what?" I ask in Hester's voice. Clear, confident. No one notices because all eyes are on Thomas, who has beads of sweat on his forehead even though it's February and it's not hot in here.

He hesitates. Electra waves her hand to urge him on.

"I'm sorry, guys," he says. A wave of anxiety starts to swell inside me. "They've pulled our funding for next year. The council has decided to sell the theatre. So this is going to be our last performance." You can hear the despair in his voice by the time he gets to the word *performance*, which he manages to whimper before disappearing backstage.

I stand there panic-stricken, rooted to the spot.

"We tried everything, but there was no way of stopping it," Electra adds, flopping down on the lopsided wooden chair that passes as an armchair in the mock sitting room created for our rehearsals.

"What about us?" the guy playing Gerald asks.

No one has time to answer because the sound system suddenly blasts on and we're assailed by a burst of shrill, piercing sounds, like electronic screams from a second-rate horror film. The volume is so loud I can feel the planks of the stage vibrating under my feet.

I put my hands over my ears.

"Jonah!" Electra calls in a tired voice. "Turn that thing off and come here!"

We're plunged back into silence, and I'm not sure what's worse. Jonah comes on stage and this makes me feel even more uneasy; he doesn't belong here. The hunchback lives in the tower and should never be seen in public.

"You need to find a new place," Electra replies. "Me and Thomas too. We've lost our jobs, the theatre, everything. The world sucks sometimes."

I start to cry.

The tears pour out, I can't stop them. Then I realise that everyone else is crying too, apart from Jonah, who keeps grinning as if all this had nothing to do with him.

I'd like to punch him. I want to scream or smash something, take it out on someone. But I hate making a scene, and Hester does too, so I scarper backstage to look for my suitcase.

I see Thomas in the shadows; he's cleaning his glasses with a tissue.

"Hey, Alek. Wait, I'll give you a lift," he says, forcing a smile. "Today's a big day for you, despite all our problems."

"No thanks. I'll go by m-myself. I need to cl-clear my head."

It's weird, because as I reply, dragging my broken suitcase out of the theatre, the tears keep coming but I don't make a sound. I'm silent, like there's just too much pain inside.

I lost my gran. I lost the house we used to live in. And very soon I'm going to lose this place too.

There's not much left to make my life bearable.

# 2

The bus drops me at the top of the road.

The road they told me to come to on the phone.

It's not much to look at. It fits in with the rest of this anonymous town, block after block of identical streets lined with soulless concrete boxes.

Scrawny trees stand out like the scatter of hairs on a bald man's head, hemmed into narrow borders at equal intervals along the street. Even the houses stand at equal distances from one another, each box bounded by a thin strip of garden and cowering in the cold light of the winter sunset.

I've no idea how long I sit there on my suitcase.

I'm aware of my phone ringing, but I don't bother to answer it.

And I'm aware that by the time I eventually get up, once I have accepted that I can't turn back the clock, that I really don't have any other option, the street lights have come on, darkness has fallen and an icy cold has settled into my bones.

I set off again, dragging my case behind me and scanning the house numbers until I get to 22.

All that's left between me and my new life are a short stretch of driveway and a brown fake-wood door with a gold doorknob. When I ring the bell five minutes later, it seems to echo all the way down the street. The door opens but there's no one behind it, as if it's been opened by a ghost. I look down and see a mini person in Spider-Man pyjamas.

He's staring at me.

I stare back.

"Who are you?" he asks. It's the first sensible thing I've heard since I woke up this morning.

Before I have time to answer, a voice shouts out from inside the house, "Matt, who is it? Is it Aleksandra?"

Footsteps sound and a tall, heavy-set woman appears. She's wearing a jogging suit, her hair is tied back. She has a strained look on her face but forces a smile as she picks up the little boy and stands aside to let me in.

"Welcome, Alek. I thought you'd be here earlier," she says. "I tried to call you. Matt's been waiting for you all afternoon."

He's hardly been waiting for me, I think. It's probably just one of those stock phrases you say to be nice. I take my first few steps into the house and the door shuts behind me. I'm in a big open-plan kitchen and lounge, just like the ones you see in American sitcoms. The smell of roast chicken hangs in the air and the sofa is littered with children's toys and books.

"Are you hungry?" the woman asks me.

"Not r-really," I reply, unsure of what to do with

myself and my suitcase. I just stand there, watching her move around the kitchen as if I were a regular guest who doesn't need to be told what to do. As if we saw each other all the time.

She stops, puts the child down and looks over at me, forcing another smile.

"How about I show you your room?"

I follow her along a hall lined with matching doors. The hallway is narrow, designed to take up as little space as possible, which makes it feel like the walls are closing in on you as you walk along.

"Here we are. It's not huge, but I hope it'll do."

I look at the long, bare room in which a bed, a desk and a swivel chair stand forlornly. It smells of still-wet paint.

"We'll get you some more furniture and some curtains this weekend – how does that sound?" the woman says, as if she's apologising. "It all happened so quickly, we only had time for the basics. But at least that means you can pick something you like."

What I'd like is to be anywhere but here.

I'd like to say to the woman, "Don't you get it? It won't work."

I'd like to say, "It's too late for all this, for the bedroom, for the roast chicken."

But I don't. I just fake a smile too. "Ok-kay."

She doesn't know where to look. A flush of embarrassment has risen to her cheeks, her eyes dart towards me then back at the walls again, as if we were in an art gallery and there was something to look at. Saying that, I'm staring at my shoes.

"My c-case is broken," I tell her, not really knowing why. "It might've sc-scraped the floor."

I don't sound like it bothers me. It comes out more as a statement.

She shrugs and says, "It doesn't matter. We gave up worrying about the house three years ago, when Matt started walking. We'll get you a new case."

The silence that follows is so heavy, I can feel it swirling around us, drowning me.

The woman realises and flushes red again, the alarm showing in her eyes. "But you won't need it again, obviously. Maybe just for the summer, the holidays," she adds hurriedly. She sighs. "Take your time to sort yourself out, then come and join us. Dinner's nearly ready."

She disappears back down that tunnel of a hall.

I'm left on my own, in a white box that is to be my bedroom. It's dark on the other side of the door. It's dark outside the window. At a loss for something to do, I push my case into the corner and open it. I run my hands over the flannel shirts on top, all dark checks, all two sizes too big. My gran bought them for me and, as I touch them, I think about her, about how she's gone.

I sit on the bed and try not to cry. I didn't even cry at the funeral, but only because I'd cried myself dry in the days leading up to it. I couldn't take any more. I wanted to tell the priest to hurry up, let my gran go quickly. It was tearing me to pieces having to look at the coffin. Yet when they threw the last of the earth onto her grave, I didn't feel relieved, just empty, and the hole inside me is still there. I've no idea when it'll heal. Maybe never.

"Will you read me a story?" a little voice asks.

I turn round and see a mini Spider-Man framed in the doorway.

I'd like to say, "Get lost, usurper."

But instead I reply, "All r-right."

He comes over, a picture book in his hands, nearly as big as him. He plonks it down on my knee and climbs up on the bed beside me. I can feel the heat of his body and his soft arm next to mine. I'd like to push him away.

"Start from here," he tells me, pointing at the page.

I start reading and tears well up, making my voice wobble, but I hold them back.

"I'm a little fish all alone," I read.

I look at the picture of the little fish with its mum and dad. I stare at it and, a few seconds later, I become the fish. Fish don't stutter. "I wish I had a friend." I sigh and turn the page. The little fish is blowing bubbles at a plump yellow duck. "If I had a friend," I read, "life would be twice as much fun."

"What's that?" Spider-Man asks, pointing at the page again.

"A duck," I reply.

"And that?" he adds, in a tone of voice that hints he could go on for ever.

"That's duck poo I th-think."

He throws himself back on the bed, giggling. He's

laughing so hard it's like duck poo's the funniest thing he's ever heard.

"Is poo funny?" I ask him, puzzled.

He's in stitches, rolling around on the bed. I don't know what to do. I could pick him up and carry him out into the hall, that way he might realise it's time to go back to the kitchen and leave me alone.

Then he hears a noise.

Keys turning in the front door.

Mini Spider-Man's ears prick up like a dog's, his eyes open wide, he jumps down from the bed and rushes to the front door shouting, "Daddy! Daddy!"

For a second I envy him. The word tumbles out so fast, in such quick succession, it sounds like a drum roll. Dad-*dy*-Dad-*dy*-Dad-*dy*. He must really love him. I have no idea what that feels like. I hear him shout, "I saw duck poo!"

I get up and close the door. I don't think I'm ready for a family dinner. And, anyway, this isn't my family.

I go over to the window and open it wide. I need air. A wintry chill hits me, bites me. I take a deep breath and try not to die, not to be sick.

Opposite mine, in the house next door, is another bedroom window and the light is on. It's so close and the hedge between the two houses so low that I can see inside. I see a girl moving about, throwing clothes around as if she's looking for something. She stops in the middle of the room, thinking. Or it looks like she's thinking.

She's blonde and is wearing something light blue. A dark-haired woman with black-rimmed glasses comes in and says something to the girl. Their shouts are muffled, but I can still make out what they're saying.

"Why can't you knock before you come in? Get out and leave me alone!"

"This is my house, don't you know?" the woman screams. "And I told you you're not going out tonight. Get that stuff off now!"

"You can't tell me what to do, bitch!" the girl yells, throwing something at the woman, a sweatshirt maybe.

"How dare you speak to your mother like that," the woman retorts, hitting out at the girl.

I move away from the window and hide in the corner so they don't see me spying on them. The girl dodged the slap and now the woman's gone. The girl runs to the door and tries to open it, failing. Her mum must have locked her in. "You're such a cow, d'you hear me?" she screams with every last bit of breath in her lungs. "I *hate* you!"

It reminds me of rehearsals, when Thomas taught us to use our diaphragms when we shout, to make our voices stronger. It doesn't sound like this girl needs any lessons. I'd like to be able to shout at people like that. I could go through to the kitchen and tell my mum the same thing – "You're *such* a cow."

Because that's what I think.

But I never say what I think. It hurts too much, more than keeping it in, and bad language wasn't allowed at my gran's house. That's why I only swear in my head, repeating the words over and over to help me stop stuttering.

The girl's by her window now, looking out.

My heart pounds and I push myself further into the wall and stretch my arm over to switch off the light.

Right away, I see her open the window, step out onto the ledge and jump down into the garden. She picks herself up, straightens her miniskirt and slinks off towards the road, silent and hunched over so as not to be seen.

I could do the same, I think, if only I had somewhere to go.

Instead I turn the light back on, shut the window and go to the door.

I don't have any choice.

I slip quietly into the hall, then shut my eyes like I do backstage, just before I have to go on. I move in the darkness, concentrating on the character I'm about to play. Then, right at the last minute, when my foot hits the stage, the spotlight turns on me and I'm ready to play the part. I become someone else.

I walk into the living room. I'm in character.

"Hey, Aleksandra. This is Luke, my ... husband," says the woman who gave birth to me, whose surname I was given. My gran's daughter.

I go over and shake the stranger's hand. My stepfather. Touching him disgusts me, but I say, "Nice to meet you."

Then I sit down at the table and let them do the talking. I let Matt move his chair to be closer to me, so close I can hardly lift my fork. I let my mother put some chicken on my plate. She won't look me in the eye, as she prattles on to her husband about the furniture we need to buy at the weekend.

I let my voice speak for itself, clear and distinct.

In character, I play out the first meal of my new life.

The first family meal with my mum since I was born.

# 3

The night my gran died, I didn't realise straight away.

She was in her armchair as usual, watching television in the living room opposite the kitchen, while I'd cleared away the dinner dishes and was studying at the table. I had the script of the play in front of me, but I was only allowed to open it after I'd done my homework.

From where I was sitting, I could see my gran's profile outlined in the bluish light of the television.

I liked that time of day, when the town would quieten down, people everywhere winding down ready for bed, and I could pretend that everything was cool, that all I had to do was study hard and behave well to earn myself a little piece of happiness.

By the time I'd packed up my books, at around eleven o'clock, Gran was asleep. She always dozed off in front of the television and it was my job to wake her and get her off to bed. But when I went over to her that night, I sensed something cold in the air – a chill that made the hair on the back of my neck stand up and seeped into my bones. The heavy white curtains in the living room fluttered, so I went straight to the window to close it. It wasn't open.

I felt my heart skip a beat, and another.

"Gr-Gran?" I called out, struggling for breath.

She didn't reply. She was just sitting there, her hands clutching the arms of her chair, her eyes closed, as if she were sleeping. She was there, but she'd already gone. I touched her hand and it felt lifeless, like a piece of limp wood.

In a state of shock, I turned round and went back to the table to read Oscar Wilde.

Everything after that is a blank. Even now, I can't piece it together. Darkness, faces, noises, images blurry through my tears, the doctor's voice as he shone a light in my eyes, our neighbour sleeping on the sofa, the phone call, my mum at the funeral, my mum telling me I had to go and live with her because I've got nowhere else to go, the curtain falling silently on me, no applause.

My gran was only fifty-nine. She cycled, she didn't smoke, she did voluntary work for the church. I'd thought I'd see her grow into a sprightly old lady, years away in the future. I'd thought she'd give me time to grow up, looking after the house, sorting out any problems, taking care of me, just like she'd been doing for as long as I can remember.

But she left me all alone, just like my mum and dad.

I wonder if that's my fate, to watch the people who are supposed to love me for ever disappear from my life. But then, how long is "for ever"? An instant, a heartbeat, just

20

long enough to realise where you are before it's all over. For ever. It's a cruel word that only seems to hold true for death. Death is for ever. Oscar Wilde would have come up with a witty one-liner to make it easier to bear. I, on the other hand, have been lying awake since 5 a.m., staring at the ceiling and watching the early morning sun slowly tinge this anonymous bedroom with colour.

I hear pint-sized footsteps running along the hall, on the other side of my closed door.

I hear a whiny voice. "I don't want to go!"

Then adult voices whispering, more steps, doors opening and closing, giggling.

Someone taps on my door but I ignore it, my body tensing under the covers. I stay in bed and wait for this burst of family life to be over. The sound of the front door, banging twice in rapid succession, fills me with a sense of relief, as if I've been given the all clear to leave my cell.

I wait for the cars to come out of the garage and drive away before I finally get up, the house now silent. There's a pile of clean towels outside my door with a note saying, "These are for you. Have a nice day, see you later."

I go through my normal morning routine on auto pilot, trying to ignore the fact that I don't belong here. There's a clean cup and everything I need for breakfast on the kitchen table. But I'm not hungry. I pick up my school bag, stuff my jacket in and run out, grabbing the new set of keys lying on the hall table with the message, "For you."

The cold winter air rouses me. I'm about to set off down the street when I hear shouting.

"Come back here now!"

It's coming from the house next door. I take a step back and linger on the doorstep, listening.

"Just piss off, will you," I hear, as the blonde girl storms out and slams the door. There's a guy on a motorbike by the gate.

"Piss off yourself," he says to her.

She sidles up to him with a smile. "I wasn't talking to you, you jerk. I meant that stupid bitch in there."

She's wearing fuchsia pink leggings and a cropped jacket over some kind of skinny black top that covers half her bum. On her feet are high-heeled black ankle boots. She really swings her hips from side to side, shaking out her blonde hair as she pulls on the helmet the biker guy has given her.

She climbs on behind him and they fly off down the street at full throttle, disappearing into the distance in a matter of seconds. The woman with the black-rimmed glasses comes running out of the house and looks around, disappointed to find her daughter already gone.

With this scene floating around in my head, I head off to the bus stop. But instead of getting a bus to school, I take one in the opposite direction, towards the theatre.

I've never been here in the morning before. I look at the name carved above the main entrance. The cream-coloured paint of the old façade is all cracked and faded. It doesn't look antique though, just decrepit. The whole town is too young to boast any kind of historic monument or building.

As soon as I smell the dust, the wood and the soft velvet of the padded seats, I feel better. I steer clear of the wings and stage, and slip into the darkness of the stalls.

I sit off to the side, trying not to be seen, and watch Thomas mess about with some props. In an attempt to save electricity the only light is coming from a bulb in the wings.

Electra comes in, draped in her usual long, loose, swirly layers.

"Are you finished?" she asks Thomas.

"Almost. I'm going to see the councillor next. Apparently I've got an appointment."

Electra pulls a face. "I'll believe that when I see it."

"I need to sort something out, at least for Helena," Thomas says. "She's the one I really worry about."

"She's not your daughter, Thomas. You have to let things take their natural course," Electra says. "Something terrible happened to her, but it's not your problem."

I cough loudly. I don't want to hear the rest.

They both jump. I see them screw their eyes up in the almost total darkness before they finally spot me.

"Aleksandra!" Electra cries. "What are you doing here at this time of day? What's happened? Are you okay?"

I get up to move closer to her, but she's already bouncing down the stairs and running towards me.

"Are you okay?" she says again.

I can see the surprise in her eyes. Quite a few of the younger ones at the Ship of Fools often skip school to come and hide here. Not me. I've never missed a day of school unless I was ill. I've never not done my homework and I've never had detention.

"I'm f-fine. I just d-didn't feel like b-being shut up in a classroom today," I reply.

"Come on then," Electra says, relief in her voice – she's back to her usual brisk self. She likes to play the grouch, but underneath all the layers she piles on to hide her bulky frame, she has a heart just as big as her body.

As soon as I go on stage, I feel calmer and start to think more clearly. For instance, I realise I should've had breakfast. I'm starving and I can't just stop eating because I'm living in someone else's house. It also occurs to me that my mum will be mad when she finds out I've skipped school. What if she doesn't want to keep me? Then I really will have nowhere to go. I feel a dark veil of anxiety settle over me.

Luckily Electra dumps a pile of costumes down beside me, and asks would I mind taking the tacking out. I don't mind.

"So, how'd it go last night?" Thomas asks, cautiously.

"Ok-kay. I've got my own room and we had chicken for dinner," I reply.

They look at me, expectant, waiting for more, but I focus on picking out the stitches from the hems of the costumes instead.

The seconds hang in the air, the silence deafening.

"I've got a brother."

"But you knew that, didn't you?" Electra asks, trying to sound offhand. I realise they're both studying me. "Your gran told you, didn't she?"

"Yes, she did. But I've really got one now, don't you see?" I say. "He was there, in his pyjamas, clinging to me."

"Well, that sounds great," Thomas says, enthusiastic now. "What's he called?"

"Matt."

It's the first time I've said his name and that unsettles me. A name is real, there's a real person behind it, or a character, maybe both, depending on what side of the stage you're on, what scene you're in, who you're playing in the show. Or in life.

"Do you want to do some improvisation?" Electra asks me, changing the subject, maybe because of the look on my face. "I have a few movements to try out. And it's freezing in here, so at least it'll warm us up. What do you reckon?"

I love improvisation exercises.

We usually do them to classical music. Electra and I stand up straight in the middle of the stage, one beside the other, arms by our sides, and start breathing deeply to prepare. We breathe in and out in time to the music, our minds following, the melody unravelling any knots. For now at least.

"Bird," says Electra, and I smile. It's one of my favourite figures. I hold my arms out and start to move, using all the space around me, acting like a bird with feathers, wings, a beak and delicate, clawed feet.

Electra does the same. It's amazing how weightless

she looks. We brush past each other, lightly, without colliding, in an improvised dance like birds soaring.

When I feel ready to change, I say, "Elephant," and we stop dead as if we were as heavy as houses, as if every movement took an enormous effort. I imagine I've got a trunk on my face. I imagine my big ears, and the savannah stretching out before me. We stamp our feet slowly on the wooden boards, swaying, moving in random patterns.

"Kangaroo," she yells suddenly, and we start bouncing around like mad.

It makes me laugh. Electra laughs too; we can't stop. My hands are out in front of me, like the short arms of a real kangaroo, and I jump around, knees bent, imagining I have a pouch on my stomach. Electra looks really funny. She's laughing and jumping about too, her clothes bouncing with her, her face flushed with effort.

Then I hear someone else laughing up above me. I stop dead in my tracks and look up, bringing a hand up to my chest, over my shirt.

I see Jonah, sitting on a rafter with a screwdriver in his hand, laughing and waving at me.

"A-a-a-" I stutter, but I can't get the word out. When I'm really angry, I get totally stuck.

"*A-ah-ah-ah staying alive, staying alive,*" he croons. "I didn't have you down as a Bee Gees fan."

"You're so not funny, Jonah," Electra says, shaking her head and patting her hair down. "Could you just change the light bulb and come down without disturbing us while we're working?"

I'm concentrating on breathing in and out. I'm thinking of the blonde girl next door. I take a big, deep breath, fill my lungs then let it all out.

"Arsehole!"

Clear as a bell.

"Wow!" Jonah exclaims, so stunned he nearly falls off his perch.

Electra bursts out laughing. "Brilliant. That was absolutely brilliant. Jonah's succeeded where we've all failed for the past three years!" she cries. "And Thomas missed it because he had to go and speak to that stupid councillor."

I start to laugh again too.

I have just uttered my first ever swear word. It feels good. It feels good seeing Jonah's face as he climbs down from the rafters to the sound of Mozart.

Just two years ago, I had to turn down the role of Jenny Diver in Bertolt Brecht's *The Threepenny Opera* because the script had words like *whore* and *screwing* in it. I didn't want my gran coming to watch and hearing me trying to say them.

But now I've managed to tell an arsehole that he's an arsehole.

Electra squeezes me tight and for a second I think that, if today really has to be the first day of my new life, then it might not be a total disaster. I might just be able to find a way of surviving as this new me.

# 4

"We can buy you some new clothes if you need anything," my mum offers, in a hesitant tone.

I'm not sure how I look to be honest. I don't like mirrors because I find it hard to look myself in the eye, and I've never bothered much with clothes. My gran always got our stuff at the market or in a discount shop near our house, and I made do with that. It was her money after all, and I was grateful for everything she was doing for me already.

"I d-don't really n-need anything," I say. I'm helping her clean the kitchen while the cake she's just made bakes in the oven.

"Your gran saw things her way," she says with a frown, still talking about clothes.

I tense up. I don't want her speaking ill of my gran, so I change the subject.

"I didn't go to school today."

She turns off the tap, dries her hands and sighs.

"Why not?"

"I didn't feel like it," I reply in a voice that doesn't

sound like mine. I don't care what she says. If anything, I wish she'd get mad, scream, tell me what she really thinks, namely that she doesn't want me any more now than she did back then, and that she's only taken me in out of pity. All of a sudden, I need to know the truth.

She thinks about it for a second, then apparently decides not to share her thoughts. I guess this being-a-mum role is new to her, given that she never brought me up and Matt is only four.

"It's not the end of the world I suppose," she finally remarks. "I realise that this move must be hard for you. If you want to take a few days off, that's fine by me."

I nod even though I'd rather disagree with her. That's not how it works, I want to yell. You're supposed to get angry, shout at me, ground me. You're the one who's meant to make the rules. I'd like to tell her that Gran never budged from her rules.

But I don't.

Instead I think about those three little words. *"If you want."*

Now there's a question.

What do I want? Now that I've lost everything?

"Think about the clothes," she says to break the silence between us. "We could go shopping together, it'd be fun."

"Okay," I reply, knowing it'll never happen.

Mum takes the tin out of the oven, sniffs it and touches the cake gently with her finger. "Perfect!" she cries. "We'll take it over to Carla's – she only lives next door and she wants to meet you. She's invited us over for coffee."

"In the h-house you c-can see from my bedroom?" I ask, wondering.

"Yes, that's it. Did you see her in the window? She's tall with black hair," she answers, turning the cake out onto a plate. She does it a bit clumsily, a bit fast, and the cake breaks as she turns it over. "She's got a daughter your age, you might've seen her at school."

"N-no, I don't think so," I say. I've never seen the blonde girl at school. Then again, I don't hang out in the same places as people like her. The library isn't the best place for socialising, given the big "Quiet Please" signs everywhere.

A few minutes later, we're out on the street, heading next door together. As we get closer, I'd like to turn round and go back inside. Being beside my mum, out in public, side by side like this, upsets me. I can barely put one foot in front of the other.

And I'm hot with embarrassment about having spied on her friend and her daughter. Worse still, when Carla opens the door and gives us such a warm reception, I'm even more embarrassed that I know what she looks like when she's angry or disappointed. Not the relaxed smile she's flashing now, but the grimace that distorts her face, making her look like she will when she's an old lady.

"Hi, Aleksandra," she cries, squeezing my hand and ushering us in. "At long last I get to meet you. Your mum's told me all about you."

The platitudes adults trot out to avoid the awkward truth fascinate me. Like, "Hi, Aleksandra. It's really weird to meet you. Your mum mentioned she'd had a child sixteen years ago, but I heard she'd managed to get rid of you."

I wonder if I'll be as good at making this stuff up when I'm an adult, if I'll be able to chat away about meaningless things, like this new rug that's just arrived from who knows where, that Carla seems a bit too excited about.

I sit down on the sofa in the open-plan lounge. It's another sitcom-set of a room like my mum's, and I listen to them chat, sipping a cup of green tea.

I hate green tea, it tastes bitter and horrible, but I drink it anyway because my mum's cake is too dry and sticks in my throat.

"I think you go to the same school as my daughter," Carla announces after a bit, addressing me for the second time. Her face clouds over. "But I bet your marks are much better than hers."

I say nothing, but my mum tilts her head to one side in sympathy. "Are things not getting any better?" she asks gently.

Carla shakes her head. "I'm at my wits end," she sighs. "I've paid three different teachers for extra tuition, but it's useless." She falls silent and stares straight through me. "She's in her room. I'll introduce you if you want."

I know that it's not a real question, so I trot after her down the narrow hall, just the same as the one my mum and her husband have in their house.

Carla knocks on a door that has music blasting out from behind it.

"Megan! Open the door, please," she shouts, banging harder.

The door hurls open. "What the hell do you want now?" the girl snaps, appearing in the doorway. Her blonde hair's tied back in a ponytail and she's wearing a vest and pants, nothing else. I look away, but it doesn't seem to bother her that's she's standing there half-naked.

Her mum, seemingly oblivious, continues, "This is Aleksandra, Lara's daughter. Maybe you two could have a chat."

Megan sizes me up. Literally. From top to toe. Then she says, "Okay, come in."

Carla nudges me inside and the door shuts behind me.

"So? What do you do?" she asks, leaving the music blaring and throwing herself onto the unmade bed. She sits up to grab a square bottle of nail polish from her bedside table and starts painting her toenails with it.

"N-nothing s-special," I reply, unable to come up with anything better.

"Do you want some?" she asks me, picking up another bottle from the table. "I don't use this one any more because sea green's my colour now. But dark blue would suit you."

She runs a critical eye over me. I take the bottle from her and fiddle with it. Should I take my shoes off now and copy what she's doing, or take the polish home with me? Anxiety starts to ripple through me, so I focus hard on the room. It's only then that I notice what a mess it is. It's an unusual kind of mess that I don't recognise right away, but then it reminds me of something I've seen before. Theatre costumes in the making. My gran sewing my dress for the school show. Threads, scraps of material, buttons, sequins, ribbons and lots of other dressmaking things scattered across the desk, on the floor, everywhere. Then I notice all the drawings pinned to the walls.

"Do you like them?" Megan asks, without looking up from her nails.

I take a closer look. They're sketches. Elongated female figures with rough drawings of dresses, accessories, shoes. They look like two-dimensional paper mannequins. "You're r-really good. Th-they're really pr-pretty," I say, meaning it.

She gets up, flings open her wardrobe and starts pulling clothes out, throwing them onto the floor.

"I made these. I draw them then I make them, see? I make bags too." She throws me a bag, in lime-green felt, and I like how it feels. It's really original, asymmetrical in shape, with a darker green handle.

"I can see it's not really your style," Megan says, pulling a face and staring at my red and black checked shirt. "Where the fuck did you get that? At a discount shop for lumberjacks?"

Her words are like a slap in the face, but I try not to let it show. "My gr-gran b-bought it for me," I say, smoothing the shirt down with my hands. The fabric pulls tight over my chest and Megan lets out a whistle. She comes over to me and stands so close I can smell her perfume. She bends over slightly and I glimpse the roundness of a breast down her vest.

"Hey, girl, what you hiding in there?" she shouts, cackling a bit too loudly.

I don't know what she's talking about. I shrug my shoulders, hoping it's the right thing to do. She takes no notice, opening her eyes wide as the next track on her playlist kicks in. She must like it a lot, because she jumps on the bed and starts singing at the top of her voice, pretending she's got a microphone in her hand. She dances around like she's in a music video, not on her bed at home, in her knickers in front of a total stranger.

"Come on, join in!" she shouts, waving her arms to get me to climb up on the bed beside her.

I shake my head. "I d-don't know how to," I say, but I feel like laughing.

She puffs out her cheeks in exasperation, jumps down and takes my arm. "Oh yes you do, baby. Even Beyoncé would move like a teddy bear in a fluffy dressing gown like that!"

She laughs and pushes the mirror into the middle of the room, practically forcing me in front of it. Then she dives into the pile of clothes on the floor and starts rummaging through them, throwing things up into the air in an explosion of colours and fabrics.

I look at myself in the mirror. My reflection looks back and says, "Where the fuck did you get that?"

"What do you think of this?" Megan cries, her reflection appearing behind me in the mirror. She's holding out a strapless dress, turquoise with a flared short skirt.

"Is it my size?" I ask. It looks way too small for me.

"We'll soon find out. Take off the dressing gown," she instructs, and she starts unbuttoning my shirt before I've had time to answer.

I recoil. "I-I'll do it," I say, smiling to cover my embarrassment while wishing my mum would come and rescue me, say it was time for us to go home.

I slowly peel off my shirt and hold it in my hand.

Megan takes a long look at me. She has me spin round, takes my shirt off me and chucks it on the floor.

"For a goody two-shoes, you've got great tits!" she cries. "There's no way this dress'll fit you. It's my size, see? I've got two tiny peaches, not killer melons like yours."

"Ok-kay, it d-doesn't matter," I splutter in relief, quickly bending over to pick up my shirt.

"Wait a minute," she chirps, darting back to the wardrobe. "I've got some material ..."

Seconds later, I'm standing in front of the mirror in my bra and pants and Megan is draping hot pink material over me. Bits of gold sparkle in a pattern along its edges. She gathers my hair up in a ponytail to get it off my shoulders and I have no idea why I let her. I give in to her enthusiasm, to the way she does things, as if she knows exactly what her place is in the world.

I glance at myself in the mirror and see my body appear and disappear under the material.

"What do you think about a '70s look? Slightly loose and flowing, the way you like, but low cut enough to show you're a woman not a lumberjack," Megan suggests.

All of a sudden, she's lost her flippant, playful expression and now she looks focused and professional, as if she really cares about making me a dress.

I nod and she gives me a thumbs-up.

"B-but I'd never have anywhere to w-wear it," I say. "I d-don't go out that m-much to be honest. Y-you'd be wasting your t-time."

"Nah ..." she says. "A dress is never a waste of time. And I like designing dresses for other people, it's a good way of trying out different styles."

With a thrust of her arm, she sweeps everything from her desk onto the floor and sits down to draw, picking out pencils from a box in front of her.

"What size are you?" she asks me.

"I d-don't know. The shirt's extra l-large, I th-think," I answer.

"No, what bra size, I mean." She stands up and pulls on my strap to check the label. "An F cup. F, would you believe it! How bloody lucky is that!"

She bounces back to her desk and starts drawing again. I stand there, not moving, not knowing what to do with myself, wondering whether I should sit down or just keep standing. I keep standing.

"What I don't get, is why you keep them hidden," she exclaims, shaking her head. Her blonde ponytail dances along. "When you get a gift like those," she nods at my chest, "the least you can do is be proud of them."

"My gr-gran didn't want me to d-draw attention to myself," I mumble.

"Listen, what's your gran got to do with it? Why do you go on about her all the time?" she asks, quickly colouring in part of her drawing. I can see the figure starting to take shape beneath her hands.

"Because I used to live with her," I say, "but she's d-dead now."

"Why didn't you live with your mum?" she asks.

Something about the way she asks makes me want to answer. It's like my past is no big deal for her, it's just something to talk about here in her bedroom, while she draws, while we get to know each other.

I take a deep breath. "M-my m-mum had me when she was very y-young. H-her and my dad wanted to m-move abroad, so they l-left me with my g-gran. My gran b-brought me up."

"Is that right? Well, you had a lucky escape. Mums are all bitches, if you ask me," Megan almost shouts, her face angry. "Mine is the biggest bitch of all."

"Sh-she should be proud of how t-talented you are," I say.

"Talented?" she says, turning round to face me. She looks confused, as if she doesn't know what I'm talking about. "What planet are you from?"

I go ice cold inside and my ears start to burn. I didn't mean to insult her, but I've obviously said the wrong thing. I hold my breath and wait for her to say she's changed her mind, she's not making me the dress any more and can I please get out her room.

She bursts out laughing instead.

37

"Come off it, they're just clothes," she says. "My mum thinks they're a complete waste of time, certainly not an art form and even less of a talent."

"She d-doesn't l-like them?" I ask, amazed, and relieved she's not offended. "My g-gran used to say that a t-t-ta-talent is a gift that can save your l-life."

"So why didn't she want you to show the world your tits?" Megan hits back, and I don't know whether it's meant to be a joke, as she's turned her back on me, is drawing again. "My mum teaches at the university and thinks that everyone should be a dull academic like her. She couldn't care less about clothes and refuses to give me any money for material."

Then she turns to show me the drawing. She's grinning proudly and I see that she's really pretty, Megan, with a girlish oval face, big blue eyes and a flawless, fair complexion. "What do you say, lumberjack? It's yours if you'll burn that shirt."

I laugh. "Okay. I l-like it."

She picks up the metal bin from under her desk and empties all the papers out onto the floor. She sets it down beneath the window, then opens the window as wide as it will go.

"Wh-what are you doing?"

"Just what I said," she answers. She grabs my shirt and shoves it into the bin, then sets fire to it with a lighter she takes from the shelf. I'd like to stop her but I'm so shocked I can't get the words out. So I keep my mouth shut for fear it'll take me till tomorrow morning to say anything.

The flames leap up around us, but Megan doesn't seem too concerned. "It must've been totally synthetic," she says, clapping her hands in glee. "Look how well it's burning!"

In a few minutes, the shirt my gran bought me is nothing but ash.

When I go home later with just my jacket on over my bra, I'm hoping my mum doesn't notice or ask me anything, as any explanation will sound ridiculous.

I go into my room, but I don't switch on the light.

I stand there and think really hard and I feel my skin get lighter, my legs get longer, my eyes turn a brighter blue. I dance around in the dark, slowly, swinging my hips and lifting my arms. For a few short seconds, I'm not Aleksandra any more, the lumberjack with the bushy hair. I feel confident in my own skin, I can shout out whatever I think, and I can dance like I'm a girl on film.

Just for a second, I'm Megan.

# 5

"Where are you going?"

"To school."

"To my school?"

"No, to big school."

"Why?"

"B-because when you're b-big that's where you g-go."

"Why do you do that funny thing when you talk?"

Matt's standing beside me, staring at me while I have
breakfast. He's been following me about since he got up,
firing off question after question. I sigh. He has a tuft of
hair sticking up. It's a bit damp so someone must have
tried wetting it or put some gel on it to pat it down. It
hasn't worked.

"I d-don't know," I admit.

I don't know why I stutter, I just do. My gran used to
say it was a good thing, that at least it gave me time to
think twice before speaking. When I was in a school play
we discovered that I don't stutter when I act. No one
could explain it. Stuttering is a psychological reaction,
apparently, mainly caused by shyness and insecurity, but

when people find out that it doesn't happen when I'm acting in front of an audience, they can't believe it. I've debunked the shyness theory, but no one has ever come up with an alternative explanation.

"Do you want to come to school with me?" Matt asks, hooking his arm through mine. "We can make dinosaurs with Play-Doh."

I shake my head and pull my arm back. "I c-can't, I'm too b-big. We d-don't play in my s-school."

"I'm never going to big school, then. Never, ever, ever ..." he singsongs, running round and round the sofa with his arms jutting out like the wings of a plane.

I wish he'd go away or at least stop shouting, but I haven't the guts to say anything to this stranger of a brother. I can't even bring myself to touch him.

Luckily, my mum's husband comes into the room, tightening the knot in his tie. "Are you ready, Mr Gruffalo?" he asks.

"I'm not a gwuffalo!" Matt shouts, clinging onto his leg, trying to bite it. Luke laughs it off, ruffling Matt's hair with a smile.

How can you smile at someone who's trying to sink their teeth into your leg?

"We're leaving now, Aleksandra," he says. I stare into my mug and nod. "After work I'll pop to the supermarket. Do you need anything? Something you used to eat at your gran's that we don't have, maybe?" he adds in a kind voice.

I'd like to say that I've got everything I need here, except my gran.

I shake my head instead, looking up and pretending to smile while staring straight ahead at a fixed point on the wall behind him to avoid catching his eye. "N-no thanks."

"Okay then. Have a nice day," he says, grabbing Matt as he finishes yet another lap round the sofa, and marching him out the door with a *vroom-vroom* noise.

It's my third day here and I've discovered I *can* actually live in this house without having to spend too much time with its inhabitants. We all have our own things to do, including Matt the little monster, who goes to school, has swimming twice a week plus his friends' birthday parties and all the rest. I never knew family life could be so hectic, maybe because me and Gran lived at a slower pace.

"Both feet on the ground and eyes straight ahead, Sandra," she used to say. Gran never used the 'k' in the middle of my name. She called me something completely different so as to prove that the girl she looked after had nothing to do with my parents and their choices. "The world's a dangerous place for the likes of us," she'd tell me. "We need to watch out. You don't want to end up like your mother."

I never really understood what she meant by that. Every time she said it, though, a shiver ran down my spine. I knew that "to end up like your mother" was a fate worse than death for my gran. It had the force of an insult. So I kept both feet on the ground, like she said, and my eyes straight ahead.

But as I'm getting dressed, I take a proper look at my clothes and I realise it's true – they're nothing like what everyone else is wearing, all the normal people. I rummage round in my case where I'm keeping my stuff until we get some furniture and pull out a couple of long-sleeved summer tops. They're all polo tops, all two sizes too big, but at least the colours are more like the ones I saw in Megan's room. I pick a yellow one with the word *Goodbye* across the front, bought at the market last year, and pull it on over my jeans. I dig out my faded white canvas sneakers and shove my scuffed and boring black boots into the corner.

By the time I get to school I'm so cold I'm shivering, but I manage to survive as far as the classroom, where I stand by the radiator to warm up.

Camilla, the girl I've been sitting next to since we were eleven, backs up when she sees me and tilts her head to the side with a questioning look about her. "What's up?"

"N-nothing. Why?"

She pulls a face and throws her backpack onto the desk. "You're going red from ear to ear. And you know it. Is everything all right with the flake?"

She started calling my mum "the flake" when I told her how she left me with my gran to make a new life for herself. I feel myself swell with pride when she says it. I like the way Camilla pronounces "flake". The word rolls off her tongue naturally, as if that's just the way my mum is, like fire is hot and the sea is salty.

"I've found a w-way of not s-spending time with

43

them," I reply, sitting down. "I c-come out of my room as l-little as p-possible. H-homework is a g-great excuse."

"Nice one. Don't give her the satisfaction."

At lunchtime, Camilla runs off as usual to music practice. She's in the local brass band and earns extra pocket money playing at town fairs and festivals, which is why she never misses practice. The same as me and the theatre, and I'm sure that's what makes us stay friends even though we only ever see each other at school.

I head to the canteen by myself, going over Hester's lines in my head, practising for rehearsals this afternoon.

*Ask your own heart, not mine. I never had a mother to save, or shame. Who, being loved, is poor? Oh, no one.*

Tray in hand, I'm about to shuffle into my usual spot in the corner, by the window, when I hear a voice calling me.

"Aleksandra! Hey, I'm over here!" the voice says. I turn round to see Megan sitting with her friends, waving her hand to snag my attention. "Why don't you come and sit with us?"

She's shouting way too loud and everyone's looking at me, so I shrink into myself and scuttle over to them as quickly as possible so that she'll stop yelling. My cheeks are so hot they're sizzling, but I let my hair fall over my face so no one will see.

"How come I've never seen you here before, in all these years?" Megan exclaims as I sit down. "Girls, this is Aleksandra. That's Anna, Dani and Kayley."

One of them gives me a look. "You're the one with the disgusting shirts, aren't you? Don't you remember,

Megan? Whenever we'd see her around, you'd always wonder how she didn't die of actual shame in those shirts."

I gape at Megan and grip my fork tight. It was a mistake coming over here. I'd like to get up and go back to where I was, but she lays a hand on my arm and smiles. "That was before, snitch bitches," she announces, laughing. "Alek and I are neighbours now and I'm making her a dress."

Dani and Kayley throw each other a sceptical look.

"You've no idea what a hot body this girl's got," Megan adds, almost prodding my chest with her fork. "She'll be amazing, you can bet on it."

Kayley sneers at me. "So what's with the name Aleksandra?"

"Hey, that's rich coming from someone with the same name as my aunt's dog," Megan chimes in, fending her off.

I've no idea why she's defending me. They're her friends and I'm no one to her. I like it, though. She's the leader of the pack and the others can't get rid of me, even though I can see in their eyes that they'd jump at the chance. It's the same look I give Jonah when he's hanging around taunting me.

"My dad is Cr-Croatian. Aleksandra is a Cr-Croatian n-name," I reply, trying to sound casual and keeping my eyes on the plate in front of me.

"R-r-really?" Dani says, imitating me, making the others laugh.

Megan laughs too and I wish I could die, that the greasy floor of the canteen would open up and swallow me, but I keep sitting there like a lemon. I know it'll pass. They'll stop eventually, as long as I keep my mouth shut and don't give them any more ammunition.

"Enough of your bitching," Megan tells them, serious all of a sudden. "Get lost. I'm sick of you airheads."

"Slut," Kayley hisses under her breath. Then she air kisses Megan on both cheeks before striding off to the other side of the canteen.

"You know where to find us," Anna adds. Dani falls in behind her, mouthing "catch you later" to Megan.

When they stand, I notice their skin-tight clothes, high heels and bracelets half way up their arms. The boys all turn to watch them go, nudging each other knowingly or whistling softly.

I can hardly breathe. I'd rather not stay here with Megan, but something roots me to the spot, probably the prospect of getting up to go and having to deal with her shouting at me to stay. Megan makes me feel awkward. Megan makes me feel interesting. The combination of the two is giving me palpitations.

"They're just a bunch of birdbrains, but you won't find much else round here," she remarks, nibbling at her lunch.

As she moves her knife, I notice a massive bruise on her wrist but I don't mention it because I'm scared of stuttering again.

"Listen, I'm working on your dress," she says, a few

seconds later. "And I've thought of somewhere you could wear it. To my birthday party, next Saturday."

She's looking at me eagerly, waiting for a reaction, so I smile. "Th-thanks. Your m-mum's not a-angry any more then?"

"My mum's always angry." She glowers. "But she knows if I don't get a party at home, I'll smash the place. I mean it too. The last time I took my dressmaking scissors to her duvet cover and patchworked all the bits together to make myself a beach bag."

She laughs like she couldn't care less and I'm not sure what to think. I don't know anything about Megan's mum, except that she didn't disappear right after giving birth to her. Clearly even that isn't enough for a happy life.

"I know, you think I'm a right bitch," Megan says after a bit. "But you don't know her. She thinks she's cleverer than me because she's got a degree and a whole bunch of letters after her name, and everyone at the university thinks she's great." She says *u-ni-ver-sit-y* in a fancy posh voice, imitating her mum I guess.

"What's wrong with that?" I hazard.

Megan throws me a dirty look. "My dad walked out two years ago and she didn't do anything to make him stay. A year later she hooked up with a younger guy. Can you even believe it?" she says, looking outraged. "Then she expects me to behave like a nun. It really pisses me off."

"And she d-doesn't care about the c-clothes you make," I add, because this upsets me too.

47

"Yeah, and that …" She nods, although she doesn't seem all that sure. "Want to know what I think? Some people are born into the right family; others end up with shit for parents. You and me, we fall into the second category, that's why I think we'll make good friends."

Megan's words make me light up inside. I realise that, for her, everything's simple. With her as my friend, maybe I could find the answers I'm looking for and sort my head out.

Any time I tried to speak to my gran about my mum and dad, and about what happened sixteen years ago, it all got so complicated. Eventually I got the message that she'd rather I didn't bring it up – there were no answers and it was better just to accept things the way they were.

For Megan everything is crystal clear. We both have shit for parents and being friends could help us shake that shit off, or at least stop it from dragging us down. I say the word *shit* in my head, over and over, and the tension leaves me in a flash.

"I want to be your friend too," I reply, and I feel ablaze with sudden happiness.

# 6

I'm standing centre stage.

The five *grandes dames* in the play are all there with me. Jonah turns the spotlight on me for my monologue; it's not a joke this time. I have a full page of script to get through without messing up.

It's the first time Thomas has given me something like this to do and I can feel the tension rising around me.

I breathe in. I feel Hester's clothes against my skin.

I feel her naivety and energy become mine.

These English *grandes dames* have cast aspersions on my homeland, a land of freedom and opportunity. A country which, in the late 19th century, is building the future and trying to ensure equal opportunity for all, regardless of social class.

I breathe out.

"We are trying to build up life, Lady Hunstanton, on a better, truer, purer basis than life rests on here."

I take a couple of quick breaths and carry on.

"You rich people in England, you don't know how you are living. How could you know? You shut out from your society the gentle and the good. You laugh at the simple and the pure. Living, as you all do, on others and by them. You have lost life's secret."

One of the *grandes dames* is starting to fidget in her seat, fanning herself with increasing frequency. I look her straight in the eye for a second, accusingly. "Oh, your English society seems to me shallow, selfish, foolish ..."

As I speak, something falls on me from above. It's only a scrap of plastic, maybe some sticky tape that's come undone, but it distracts me all the same. I can't feel Hester's dress any more. My confidence melts away.

"It h-has b-blinded its eyes, and s-stopped its ears ..." I stop, bite my lip and mumble, "S-sorry."

"You were doing really well. But don't worry, the more you rehearse, the more confident you'll be and you won't even have to think about the words," Thomas says to reassure me, but I catch the look of disappointment on his face.

The scene continues without any more hiccups. I get my concentration back and focus on the words that have to come out smoothly, like silk, like water. No creases, no rocks. I breathe in and out, keeping pace with the play right to the end, even though I messed up an important monologue.

When we stop and the others scatter, I scour the stage until I find what it was that broke my concentration. It's a little piece of black plastic; a funny shape, not something I recognise. I stick it in my pocket and look up, but Jonah's gone.

While everyone gathers round the cakes and flask of coffee that Electra always brings, I head to the bathroom. At the last minute, I slip into the costume room, holding the door so it doesn't creak, so no one will notice me. Over against the back wall, behind a line of puffy dresses hanging on a rail, I spot the big boxes of shoes, piled on top of each other, and I pull out one with my size marked on it.

I rummage around, pushing aside the Arabian Nights slippers, the ballet shoes and the tango dancing shoes until I come across some ordinary black ones with heels that aren't too high.

I yank off my trainers without unlacing them and try the heels on, looking at how smart my feet look in them. I try to imagine what they'll be like with the dress and if this is what Megan meant by "get yourself some decent shoes".

"What are you doing, Lady Hester?"

A voice startles me. "It's n-none of your business. L-leave me a-a-alone."

"Okay, no worries, I get it. Peace, sister," Jonah says, laughing. I'm sitting on the floor and he seems enormous from down here. He's tall, too tall. He's staring at me and doesn't look like he has any intention of going away. "Nicking shoes, were we?"

I hurry to take them off, averting my eyes from his sniggering face.

"N-no," I reply, rising to my feet. "I-I'm b-borrowing them."

Even when I stand up, I still only come up to his chest.

I stare at his faded T-shirt with *Drop Out* written across the front.

"L-let me p-past."

"Wait," Jonah says, barring my way. He moves towards me and I take a few steps back until I feel myself come up against the rail of dresses and can retreat no further. "I want to ask you something."

He's looking at me with that wonky smile of his and he seems to be studying me. I can feel his eyes all over me and I wish I still had my thick flannel shirt on and not this top that I'm shivering inside.

He's so close I instinctively reach out to try and get him away from me. I'm pushing with all my might, but he doesn't budge an inch.

"Take it easy, Lady Hester," he says, amused. He grabs my wrists. "I'm not going to eat you. How about we ..."

I don't want to hear any more. I can't bear it. I hate him. I think of Megan, the burning bin in her bedroom and how she clapped her hands in glee over the fire. I gather every ounce of my strength and launch myself at Jonah, lifting my knee and aiming it between his legs.

I hit him almost without realising it.

He falls to the ground groaning, releasing my hands to cup his own to his groin. I take the chance to push past him and flee out of the door.

"Have you gone totally mad?" he yowls from the floor.

I run into Thomas by the dressing rooms. "Why's Jonah yelling?" he asks, looking surprised. "Why are you running? What's going on?"

"Nothing. I'll see you tomorrow," I reply, hurrying past. I'm still in my socks; my trainers are in the costume room. I'm not going back. Outside the theatre entrance, I throw the black shoes down on the ground and shove my feet in.

Who knows how I'll make it home. Every ten steps I go over on the heel and it feels like everyone's looking at me. My feet ache and as soon as I get to the gate, I lean against the wall to catch my breath.

Megan's birthday party is in two hours.

I don't know if I want to go.

These shoes, I don't know if they're really me, and not just because I borrowed them without asking Thomas and Electra. They would've given me them anyway, but I didn't want them to know because they would've made a big thing about it. Aleksandra swore. Aleksandra's wearing high heels. When other people think you're a bit odd, every little thing you do gets blown up out of proportion to be labelled as "progress" or an "issue".

In either case, you're the centre of attention and having everyone's eyes on you just makes you want to run away, either in real life or in your imagination, it doesn't matter which.

Maybe that's why the mad stay mad. If they were to start behaving normally, the weight of people's amazement would be too much to bear.

I want to say, "Leave us alone."

I look over my shoulder and I see my mum's house.

A cold feeling overwhelms me. I miss my gran and

her tiny flat where I never felt like an oddity, a piece of mismatched furniture, even though I slept on a sofa bed.

There's a light on in the window overlooking the lane and I picture my mum working at her laptop on the kitchen table. Matt playing on the floor. His dad on his way home from work, just about to put his key in the door and set off the usual "Daddy's home" celebrations.

The image repels me and pushes me to make a decision. I move away from the wall and head over to Megan's house. All of a sudden, her party seems less painful than hiding in my room to avoid the Happy Families scene playing out like a Disney fairy tale, a scene which I'd only be interrupting.

I can already hear the blaring music out here in the lane, some kind of dance rhythm with female vocals.

"*Hola, chica bonita!*" Megan yells on opening the door. She's in pants and a T-shirt as usual, cotton wool between her toes and big fat curlers in her hair. "Come in, operation make-up is in full swing."

The open-plan living room is ready for the party; there's a buffet on the table and bottles are lined up on the kitchen worktops. "Happy Birthday Princess" banners are strewn everywhere and an enormous bunch of flowers sits on the side table by the sofa.

"My boyfriend sent me those," Megan announces, doing a half-pirouette and pointing to the bouquet.

"Hey, gorgeous!" Dani shrieks from the hall. "The straighteners are ready and Kayley's waiting for you. Get a move on."

"Okay, I'm coming," Megan trills. "You will take care of Aleksandra, won't you, darling?"

Dani shrugs. "Whatever." She looks me up and down. "Nice vintage shoes you've got there. Where did you get them?"

"They w-were a p-present," I answer, following her into Megan's bedroom which is even more of a mess than last time, believe it or not.

"Take your kit off and try this on," Dani orders, pulling something off the back of the chair and throwing it at me. "Who knows how you managed to persuade Megan to make you a dress – well done you."

It's supposed to be a compliment, but the way Dani says it and the look in her eyes grate on my skin like sandpaper. I feel so alone that every word, every gesture, stings.

I grab the dress before it hits the floor and am struck by how soft and smooth the fabric is. I try to smile at the bright colours. I think how nice it was of Megan to invite me and that maybe tonight I'll make some friends, find a place to be happy.

I undress, trying to disappear into the corner because Dani, gum in mouth, is watching me and I wish she wouldn't.

"Did you steal those knickers off your gran?" she comments, throwing herself onto the bed. She grabs a mirror and a pair of tweezers from the bedside table and starts plucking her eyebrows with the poise and precision of a surgeon.

"Yes," I reply. "What I mean is, no, I didn't steal them. We were the same size."

She stops chewing and glares at me. "Don't get smart with me."

I don't understand. I'm not being smart. But I think it's probably best not to reply, and so I pull the dress over my head instead. The room turns hot pink around me for a second and I think how nice it would be to stay like this for ever, suspended between the party and not-the-party. But then my head pops back out into the real world and I'm in a dress that's not me, with a friend who's not mine, in a room I've only been in once before. I stay on my feet and bend my head forward, trying to work out what I look like and take in the smooth pink fabric clinging to my body. I keep running my hands over the dress, lightly, as if it were something precious.

"Isn't it p-pretty?" I say. "Megan's really talented."

Dani sniggers and turns round. "Oh yes, she's got talent all right," she quips then adds abruptly, "Do you want to see yourself in the mirror or not? If you keep your head down like that you'll turn into a hunchback."

She goes back to her plucking and I move over to the mirror.

A lump rises in my throat and I feel close to tears. It's me, Aleksandra. But not the one I know.

I realise a dress can't really change you, not deep down, but the mirror's telling a different story. It's saying, *I was waiting for you*. I smile and do a half-twirl to check my profile, and the dress floats around me as if I were on the bottom of the sea. It's a simple tunic dress with wide sleeves cropped at the elbow and a straight neck, but to me it feels like ballgown.

"You need to put tights on," Dani says, her tone indifferent.

I nod and, all of a sudden, I don't know what I'm doing. Am I ready? I've no idea. The others are busy doing things I know very little about and which I wouldn't have the equipment for either.

"It is a b-bit early, isn't it," I think out loud.

"You don't think that's you ready, do you?" Dani retorts. "As soon as I'm done here, it's your turn."

Oh.

Megan and Kayley come over too and I let them get on with it. I don't have much choice. It's too late to back out now and I don't want to offend Megan after all the work she put in, making me the dress. They pluck my eyebrows even though I'd rather they didn't; it's excruciating and brings tears to my eyes. They run a shaver up my legs that tugs out the hairs and has me screaming in pain, although I only shriek out loud the once. After that I bite my tongue so they won't look at me like I'm from another planet.

They get me to take the dress off again so they can shave under my arms. Then they force me to lie down on the bed so they can rub cream into my legs. Their hands are quick and expert, tickling me, but not the kind of tickling that makes you laugh. Megan laughs though, like I'm her doll and she's playing with me.

She squirts me with perfume, hair spray, setting spray, and doesn't notice the air's getting so thick you can hardly breathe. She starts on my make-up, tilting my face with her hands and telling me to look up, look right, look left, using big pencils, smaller pencils then tiny pencils. She has a really firm hand and hardly notices my mumbling protests, the *mmmm*, *mmmmm* I murmur as she swipes lipstick over my lips.

All three of them push me in front of the mirror and start shrieking. They're acting as if they were at a show or something, but it's only me they're looking at.

"I told you!" Megan crows.

She hugs me from behind and her hands touch my chest. I freeze for a second but then think that maybe there's no need to be embarrassed when you're with friends. So I don't pull away and smile instead. I'd like to tell her "thanks". But I'm too overcome and I'm afraid I might stutter. I've never been to a party before. I don't know what we're supposed to do. But I can't tell them that. I don't want them to laugh at me, not now that I look like one of them and they seem to respect me.

"Hey girl, it's your turn now," Megan whispers in my ear. "Tonight's show night, and you're going to be a star."

I nod, relieved. "Okay."

I know what she's talking about. Going on stage is easy for me.

I just need to get into character. Once I know what character I'm supposed to be playing.

# 7

I'm on my own in a corner of the living room; I picked
the darkest one. I've got a full glass in my hand, which
Kayley gave me more than half an hour ago. I've tasted
what's in it but it's so bitter and strong I almost spat it
out on the floor. Luckily, I managed not to and swallowed
what I had in my mouth down in one go, like a big lump
of dry earth.

The room's in semi-darkness, the music's loud, every
empty space on the floor is full of people, even the sofas,
chairs, doorways. There's no way of getting through them
without having to push through groups of people or
kissing couples.

Megan, Kayley, Dani and Anna are dancing in the
middle of the makeshift dance floor and a group of
boys – all much older than us – are crowded round them,
clapping and nodding in approval.

They tried to get me to join in, but I didn't feel up to
it, and not just because I don't think I can dance. The
dress I'm wearing is gorgeous but it creeps up too much
when I move. I think I know what Dani meant, now,

when she said I should get a pair of tights. Something that would cover my legs and let me walk around without worrying about everyone being able to see my underwear. I decide not to sit down to avoid the embarrassment of it.

So, this is a party.

My gran stopped sending me to birthday parties when I started high school. She said that it all started there, at parties, and it was all because of women's lib, free love and all that. She also used to say that women will never be truly equal as long as they're the ones who conceive and have children. I've no real idea what she meant, but it was obvious it had to do with my mum and the party where she met my dad.

I'm thinking that standing here like a statue isn't much fun, but at the same time it's kind of lucky that no one seems to have noticed I'm here, when the front door swings open and three guys come in, causing a bit of a stir.

It's weird because, amid the bedlam of the party, there's a sudden absence of movement. People stop talking and dancing and look round at the three guys. One is Megan's boyfriend; she goes over to him and throws her arms round his neck. He gives her a half-smile, pushes her away and heads over to the drinks table in the corner, throwing his leather jacket over the back of a chair.

The other guy is short, balding and too old to be at a party with sixteen-year-olds, but no one seems to notice.

Even in the dark, I can tell the third one is different

from the other two. He's wearing a suit jacket over a shirt and has the kind of old-fashioned poise that guys don't have these days. His hair's chestnut brown, a bit wavy and longer at the back, and he has a perfect face. He's smiling. He seems very popular. Everyone goes over to say hello, patting him on the back, milling round him as if he were some kind of celebrity.

I take another sip of whatever's in my glass and lean against the wall, wedging myself between the TV unit and the window.

I'd like to go over and tell Megan, "Thanks for the invite, it's been a great party, but I really have to go home now."

But to go over to Megan would mean crossing the room in these heels and this gravity-defying dress, pushing my way through the crowd around her and speaking to her in front of the guy in the suit jacket, who right now is planting a smooth kiss on each cheek and wishing her a happy birthday. I realise that I feel more flustered by him than anything else.

I stand rooted to the spot and think about time. About how long a minute, an hour, a party can last. About how big you feel when you're in the wrong place trying not to be noticed. The harder you try to disappear the bigger your body seems to become.

"Hey, darling!" a voice says right next to me. I look up and see Megan's smiling face. "Come out of your corner a minute," she shouts. "I want to introduce you to someone who thinks you're cute." Then she's grabbing my arm and dragging me over to the kitchen. Unable to resist as she pulls me through the throng, I grit my teeth, try not to fall over and pray that the skirt of my dress stays down. I smile, because it seems like the right thing to do and, as Thomas says, the best way not to be noticed in a crowd is to behave like everyone else.

"Here she is, our Aleksandra," Megan exclaims, stopping in front of the third guy. "This is Ruben."

She vanishes without saying another word, leaving me panicking with this stranger who's smiling as if he knows me.

"Hi there," he says, holding out his hand. I shake it. It's cool, soft, nice. "Megan insisted I meet her gorgeous new friend and I couldn't say no. You know what she's like."

"Y-yeah, I kn-know."

He doesn't bat an eyelid when I stutter.

"Are you at college with Megan?" he asks me.

"Y-yes."

I'm answering in single-syllable words and the glass in my hand seems to weigh a ton.

"How old are you?" he asks next.

"S-sixteen," I reply, wishing I could get at least one non-stuttering syllable out.

"You look older," he comments. "Maybe it's because you look different from Megan's usual friends."

I wonder if that's a compliment. Megan's usual friends are surrounded by boys and they're dancing, looking completely relaxed. I'm not relaxed and I don't know how to dance. Maybe it's not a compliment after all.

"Do you fancy a drink?" he asks after an embarrassing silence. He takes the glass out of my hand and sits it on the kitchen counter behind him. For a second, his fingers brush against mine and my instincts don't tell me to pull away. "This'll be warm by now. What would you like? A beer or a cocktail?"

I'd like to say neither. "B-beer, th-thanks," I reply. I've never tried it, but I know the cocktail will probably be bitter and revolting all over again.

Ruben takes two beers out of the fridge, snaps them open and gives one to me. He nods at me to follow him and heads off towards the sofa, where there's only space for one.

"Wait here just a second," he tells me. "If you don't mind?"

When I sit down, pulling at my dress with my free hand, he stops and looks at me. I feel a weird shiver for a second. Then he's gone and is already on the other side of the room with Megan's boyfriend.

They're mumbling to each other, unsmiling, and it looks quite serious. I realise I have to stop staring at Ruben and suddenly notice how useful having a beer in my hand is.

I sip my new drink which, unlike the cocktail I had before, is fizzy and light. It's still bitter though. I hold my breath and swallow a few sips so I don't have to taste it, and right away I feel better, maybe because the beer's cold and it's so warm in here.

The couple next to me are stuck so close to each other

63

I can't tell which one's which in the tangle of arms and legs. She doesn't seem bothered that her skirt has ridden up into the danger zone and I can see a hand moving upwards along her thigh.

I sit still and hope they don't notice me, trying not to look at them even though it's not easy. When they come up for air, I notice that he's the old bald guy who came in with Ruben and Megan's boyfriend. And the girl who resurfaces is actually Anna, adjusting her bra. She's got a weird look on her face but she smiles. The bloke gets up and moves away, and she does the same, following him into the hall, swaying her hips. Ruben throws her a look as she sways past and, for a fleeting second, it provokes an unexpected stab of jealousy.

And then, suddenly, someone turns the music up full blast; it's a wild version of 'Happy Birthday'. Megan appears with a massive cream cake and puts it on the table in front of me. I count the sixteen tall candles glowing on it. People start to crowd round us, although plenty more don't bother moving. Megan closes her eyes and her face changes, she relaxes, as if in that dark world she can see all sorts of magnificent scenes in which her wish, the one she's about to make, comes true.

She blows the candles out and someone claps their hands. Dani comes up behind her, plunges her fingers into the cake, pulls off a huge chunk and sticks it in her mouth with a defiant look burning in her eyes.

"Silly tart!" Megan shouts, laughing. She grabs a piece of cake too and throws it at Dani, who doesn't even try to dodge it, instead smearing it all over her neckline like sun cream. Then people notice what's going on and egg the two girls on with shouts and comments I only half understand, the music's still too loud. Then it changes and a dance track comes on.

A boy goes over to Dani and starts licking the cream off her shoulders, resting his hands on her hips. She raises her arms and lets him get on with it, still dancing as if nothing has happened.

It's like a green light.

Cream starts flying everywhere. Megan rubs it over Kayley and Kayley does the same to Megan. Other girls join in too, laughing and letting the guys eat cake and cream off them.

The atmosphere turns electric and even if I'm embarrassed by how over-confident my new friends seem – or maybe I'm just jealous – I start to laugh, too. I put my beer bottle, now empty, on the table and enjoy the scene with a much lighter head. Megan picks up a chunk of cake and looks at me. I raise my hands but she doesn't seem to understand that I mean, no, I don't want to join in.

Ruben appears and slips in between us to protect me.

"Oh, leave her alone," he says firmly.

Megan puts down her weapon and heads back to the dance floor to play with the others. A couple of girls who've slipped in the cream are now rolling around on the floor laughing.

"Are you having fun?" Ruben asks, sitting down beside

me. He has to speak right into my ear to be heard over the noise, and I feel his breath brush against my neck, smell his lovely manly smell. I nod. "Megan told me you act in the theatre."

I smile and dare to open my mouth, leaning closer to his ear. "Y-yes. I l-love it."

"Me too," he says. "I go all the time with my parents. Who's your favourite playwright?"

"Oscar W-Wilde."

"Ah." He nods. "I enjoy Beckett, although I don't always get what he means."

We both laugh because we realise we're thinking the same thing.

"Another heavenly day!" I recite from *Happy Days*. "Ah yes – Good Lord! – Good God!"

"Cool," he says, impressed. "I can't remember a single line from that play. And you need a good memory to be a student."

"What are you studying?" I ask, interested.

"I'm at university," he proclaims. "Law." I sense a hint of sarcasm. "You know, my parents are both lawyers so it was the natural choice. But I'm useless at remembering all those laws." He laughs to himself then asks me, "What's the last thing you saw at the theatre?"

My ears start to burn. I take a deep breath to keep hold of my consonants. "I act b-but I've n-never been to see a r-real play."

Ruben stares at me, deep in thought. I lower my eyes, wishing I still had a bottle in my hand to give me something to do, something to hide my despair. Who's ever heard of someone who loves theatre but has never been to see a play? Only a saddo like me would be that someone. Ruben's working it out for himself and it won't be long before he comes up with an excuse to get rid of me.

What he actually says is, "Do you want to get some fresh air? There's too much commotion in here to talk." He gets up and holds out his hand to me. I take it and let him pull me up. My feet feel like they lift off the ground, just a fraction, just for a second, and I feel dizzy. Ruben leads me outside, still holding my hand, and I feel like I'd let him take me anywhere right now.

We sit down next to each other on the step. It's cold but I don't really feel it. My dress slides further up and I try to straighten it out, with little success. The world is dancing and twinkling in front of my eyes, and so I decide that it doesn't matter. After all, there's only Ruben and he doesn't seem to be looking at my legs. He's looking into my eyes. He's beautiful.

"Are you cold?" he asks me. He takes off his jacket and lays it over my shoulders, as if he were immune to the winter. I feel the fabric embrace me, still warm from his body, and I smell his smell again. "You're really pretty, you know."

I don't know what to say. I know it's not a question, but even as a compliment it doesn't sound right. I'm not pretty. Ruben is just being kind.

I swallow hard. "Th-thanks," I manage to stammer out.

"I'd like your first time to be with me, at the theatre," he continues. He's right beside me and our arms are touching. "I could take you to see a play with me. What do you think? Would you like that?"

He touches a lock of my hair at the side of my face, and plays with it in his fingers. At this precise moment, I'm on the moon, shining down through the icy black sky. I'm in a dimension that doesn't exist in the real world. My head won't stop spinning and Ruben's touch makes it spin faster. I try to get control of myself because I'm not sure exactly what I'm doing with this stranger, but a little voice in the back of my head is saying, *Go on, if you want to.*

"Yes," I reply. I can hardly breathe. "That w-would be f-fantastic."

"I like you a lot, Aleksandra," he says.

"You d-don't know m-me," I say, as if warning him, as if to put him on guard. He smiles, amused, moving his fingers from the lock of hair he's still holding to touch my face.

"We've got plenty of time for that."

I instinctively close my eyes.

A car drives up, shining its headlights at us, then turns into the driveway leading to the garage. It spoils the moment and leaves me like an ugly frog, waiting in vain for a kiss to turn me into a princess.

"That must be Megan's mum," Ruben says, standing up all of a sudden. "The party's over."

We go back inside, but Ruben's busy with his friends

and we don't get another glimpse of each other. A rumour has gone round that the owner's back and the guests start to disperse.

I see Ruben as he's about to leave with Megan's boyfriend and the old bald guy. "See you soon then," he says.

I'd like to say, "Don't go."

"Yes," is what I say instead.

It's only later, after he's left on his motorbike, after Megan's mum has freaked out about the cream everywhere and Dani, Kayley and Anna have scarpered leaving their best friend on her own, that I realise I don't have Ruben's number and I didn't give him mine.

I'd like to talk to Megan about him, but she's in tears on the floor, trying to wipe it with the cloth her mum threw at her.

I give up and go over to help her.

# 8

I can't concentrate.

For me, that means stammering after thoughts I can't hold onto.

Normal people manage to think about their own business *and* interact with the rest of the world at the same time.

You see them smiling and chatting with friends and maybe thinking, 'I have to go to the dentist today. I wonder if it'll hurt?'

That's the way normal brains work. Not mine.

My thoughts just keep coming at me and when I try to stop them, tame them and get them out in the right order, I stutter.

I repeat every consonant twice, like I'm buying time to be sure that what I'm about to say makes sense.

I remember that I started stammering when I was six, my first year in proper school. The teacher would ask me something and I'd struggle to answer. It was like a weight pressing on my stomach, suffocating me and forcing me to pronounce the words almost without breathing.

I felt like what I wanted to say wouldn't be what people were expecting me to say.

When my gran asked me, "Are you ready to eat?" it would send me into a panic. I'm not hungry, I'd think, my ears going red. But if Gran's made something, she'll be upset. Then again, if she hasn't made anything, she'll think I'm too demanding and spoilt.

Five minutes to answer an easy question. Gran would always just decide for me and stick a sandwich, a piece of toast or a slice of cake in front of me. By then, of course, I'd eat anything without argument.

My stammer wasn't an issue for Gran. "Your mother always had a big mouth and look where it got her," she used to say all the time.

My mum's a journalist for a local television station, so her big mouth must've come in handy at some point, but Gran still wasn't happy. Gran was never happy. Every now and then when I'm lying on my bed and can't get to sleep because I miss her so much, I think maybe she went away early because she wasn't happy in this world. And I think that was probably all my fault. After the disappointment of her daughter, she got landed with an insignificant granddaughter. It's not easy to bounce back from knocks like that.

I dry my tears on my shirt sleeve. I'm sitting on the edge of the bath and I can't stop crying. I've been hiding in here for half an hour. The day got off to strange start with a weird feeling I had when I woke up this morning. I kept thinking back to the party. And then, at school,

I couldn't get Ruben's face out of my head. For the first time in my life, I couldn't follow the lesson and it felt like I was in another world, unable to decipher the sounds coming out of the teachers' mouths. I was so far away I couldn't focus on the sums we were supposed to be doing during maths. I failed a class test, and thinking about this makes me cry even more. I feel like I've let my gran down. She expected perfection at school.

The truth is, I don't understand what's happening to me. It's a feeling of ecstasy that hurts, an obsessive thought that both comforts and confuses me. I can't calm myself down.

I rinse my face for the hundredth time, but the cold water can't wash away Ruben's face. His bright eyes, his chestnut brown hair curling gently behind his ears. His slim, confident hands.

I open the door to go and hide in my bedroom, maybe try to sleep, but it's full of people I don't know. Men in overalls are carrying in big boxes and I remember that yesterday was Sunday and we went to buy furniture for my bedroom.

I hear my mum's hesitant voice behind me. "You'll finally feel a bit more at home, I hope," she says. "You picked some really nice things."

I've no idea what she's talking about. I can hardly remember anything about yesterday. For the most part, I waited for Ruben to call, clinging onto my mobile all day. I was sure he would get my number from Megan because he'd said, "See you soon," and seemed to mean it.

The workmen have unpacked the furniture and started assembling it. I smell the cardboard and pretend-wood. I hear them drilling holes in the walls for the shelves. The constant *bang-bang* of the hammer reminds me of Helena and I remember I've got rehearsals today. I'm late, and my head is pounding.

"I'll drive you there if you want," my mum says when she sees me panicking. She peers at me like she doesn't understand how serious the situation is, but wants to help all the same. I feel obliged to accept the lift and feel even worse, because I'd promised myself never ever to be a burden to her. But if I get there late, the others won't be able to start without me. Or they will start, replacing me for the first time, and I couldn't bear that. Hester's my part, I don't want anyone else reading my lines, and no one's going to take her away from me.

"I'm so happy you've made friends with Megan," my mum says as we drive through a series of anonymous streets, all alike.

I'm thinking, maybe I should ask her for Ruben's number. Maybe. Maybe. Maybe.

"Carla's worried about her but I think she's a nice girl really," my mum continues. "She's just a bit of a rebel, but who isn't at that age? I'm hardly one to judge."

I can't call him, I think. I can't. I wouldn't even be able to get my name out over the phone.

"You could be a good influence on her," my mum insists, totally unaware that I'm not listening. "You're so mature."

I've entered an unfamiliar new world and I feel sick. So sick I wish I could step out of my skin and run away from myself, leaving all these overpowering feelings behind. I'm so certain that Ruben won't call me that the pain of having lost him is too much to bear. There's no point beating myself up about it. I realise I only spoke to him for ten minutes. I understand he was just being nice and complimented me like that in the dark, without really seeing me.

But that doesn't make it any easier. My brain is ignoring all that and focusing on just one sentence. *See you soon.*

"It's here, isn't it?" my mum asks when we stop at the traffic lights. I manage a nod. "What is it you're working on exactly?"

"*A Woman of No Importance,*" I reply. "By Oscar Wilde."

She stops in front of the theatre and I mumble my thanks as I get out. I hear that she doesn't move off right away; she's waiting for me to go in.

As soon as I reach the backstage area, I see Jonah sitting on a chair and Helena behind him with a pair of scissors in her hand. It looks like they live here.

"H-hi," I mumble.

He lifts his head, sees me and grabs the lid off the bin beside him. He holds it over his groin, like a shield, and squawks, "Okay, you can come over now, murderer."

Helena smiles at me. That's unusual, she never smiles. She takes Jonah's head and yanks it up, then forces him to bend his neck again. There's hair on the floor around their feet. Little blond tufts lying there like commas fallen off a script.

Helena's cutting. I've noticed that whatever tool she uses, she's always really good with it. Watching her relaxes me – except when she's hammering, that is. I sit down not too far away and observe them. Jonah's long straight hair gets clipped in satisfying short, sharp strokes. Every tuft that falls to the floor leaves his head looking neater, revealing a bit more of his hard, pointed face, straight nose, straight lips and small ears.

Unconsciously I touch my own hair, which reaches almost down to my waist.

Then I look at Helena. She's absorbed. She's determined. I'd like to ask her to cut away all my worries.

I say, "W-would you d-do mine too?"

They both look at me. There's a light in her green eyes as she nods.

Jonah, on the other hand, gets stuck in again. "Oh, so now your gran's not here to supervise, you've decided to live it up a bit?"

Helena clouts him on the back of the head and forces him to sit up straight.

"What's with the girls in this group?" he moans. "Have you all got your period at the same time? Why don't you warn us blokes? That way we'd just stay away and keep out of trouble. Easy."

Thomas comes over from the stage. "Are you going to be long?" he says. "We'd like to start."

Helena shakes her scissors at him.

He raises his hands. "Okay, I get it, I'm going. Whenever you're ready, I'm over there."

It takes a couple more minutes to finish the haircut then Jonah gets back to his feet. I'm always really surprised by how tall he is and I stand up right away so he won't tower over me.

Without saying a word, I go and sit in the seat in front of Helena. She wets my hair with a plastic spray bottle and I feel the drops tickle my ears and cheeks and land on my hands.

Jonah has gone over to the mixing deck and is messing about with the buttons. The audio kicks in and music starts to play, guitar sounds conjuring up the voices and rhythms of another era. I listen to the words – *you become an image / it cuts like a blade / a quick cut.*

I feel the cut on my skin, the one Ruben's face has left in my head.

I shut my eyes and Helena starts chopping at my hair. I don't tell her how much to cut off. I let her decide and take the weight of decision off me, along with this head of hair that no one's touched in five years.

*And all that's left / of this city / is suitcases, winter and tears.*

This song is talking to me. Jonah plays it again as Helena layers my hair. I can feel her trying to give it a less random shape.

"Wh-where did you learn?" I ask her distractedly.

"Her mum's a hairdresser," Jonah replies with a sigh. "Welcome to our world, space woman."

"Why do you never use my name?" I retort in anger. For some strange reason, just being near him makes me angry. I wish he'd go away and I'm almost happy – just for a second – that the group has to disband. At least I won't have to see him every day.

"I only call my close friends by their name," he answers. "And yours is like a swear word with its 'k' in the middle."

"You d-don't have close f-friends," I manage to say. "You're always in here."

Helena starts cutting quicker. I think this means she's enjoying our conversation; it feels like she's encouraging me to wind Jonah up. Maybe he gets on her nerves too.

"Thanks for the clarification," Jonah says. He's not joking this time. I open my eyes and see him let out a big, lonely sigh. In silence. Then he turns round and strides purposely towards me. I stiffen and dig my fingers into the edge of the chair. He goes past me, bends over, picks up the spray bottle and points it at my nose.

"Water's good for plants," he says, "especially weeds like you."

Then he sprays me. The haze of water hits me. Helena stops and pulls back. I jump up from the chair but Jonah's behind me, still spraying. "Murderer. This is for the kick you gave me on Saturday. I had to put my balls in plaster."

Over the hissing of the spray, I hear Helena let out a quick but clear laugh, then Thomas rushes over, alarmed, to sort us out. "Why do you two have to argue all the time?" he says, dramatically.

"We're not arguing. She was just a bit too dry."

When Jonah stops, I'm damp and cold, but I feel like I've calmed down. The weight in my head has gone. I realise that my hair feels lighter. I touch it and discover that it only just reaches my shoulders now, and I feel unwell. I'm going to be sick. I want to scream. But I don't, I sit back down calmly, concentrate on my breathing and let Helena put the final touches to it. To let me know she's finished, she gives me a pat on the head which at the last moment turns into a little push.

I go over to the mirror in the corner and she follows me, although she doesn't step into my reflection.

I look better, much better. You can see my face, the contours of it, my straight nose, my neat ears. Some of my worries have in fact been cut away with the hair now lying on the floor. I smile and on impulse, with no time to stop myself, I give Helena a hug. She stiffens and I think, body language doesn't stutter.

I pull away immediately. "S-sorry. Th-thanks. I-it's p-perfect."

She turns round and walks away. I see her pick up her tool belt and head off into the corner where she's working on the scenery. I wait for her to start hammering frantically, but she picks up some sandpaper instead and starts rubbing the wood patiently and rhythmically. She's not upset.

I forget Aleksandra during rehearsals.

I want to be Hester. I'm so happy Gerald loves me.

I recite one of my lines with tears in my eyes and everyone thinks I'm acting. I am. I'm not.

"Hearts live by being wounded," I recite. "Pleasure may turn a heart to stone, riches may make it callous, but sorrow – oh, sorrow cannot break it."

Thomas claps his hands and mouths to me, "Perfect! Perfect!"

I'm exhausted by the end. I'm back in my own body, Aleksandra again. The cold in the theatre wraps round me, taking me by surprise, freezing the beads of sweat on my forehead. I'm short of breath and Electra lays a towel on my shoulders.

"Well done, Aleksandra," she murmurs, pride in her voice.

I go to the bathroom and throw up, trying to be quiet so no one hears. A few minutes later I'm out in the street, standing under the lamp-post by the bus stop, when my mobile rings in my pocket. I pull it out but don't recognise the number on the display. I hesitate. Hester has snatched me out of my strange new world and I don't know if I want to go back.

The phone keeps ringing and ringing. The woman next to me stares at it, probably wondering why I'm ignoring it.

In the end, I answer in a puff of breath that rises like a cloud into the cold night. "H-hello."

"Aleksandra, is that you?"

It's Ruben.

# 9

"Keep still," Megan orders me.

I'm so excited I can't stop twitching as she comes towards me with a pair of red-hot straighteners in her hand.

"Do we really need to?" I ask, nervously.

"Oh, yes," she replies, straddling my legs.

Her weight keeps me anchored to my seat in her bedroom. Her face is just inches from mine. I notice a scratch on the side of her cheek.

"How did you do that?" I ask.

"Oh, it's nothing. I picked a spot, that's all," she replies. "Just keep still and we'll sort out that haystack you call hair."

She sits almost on top of me and works away patiently, taking a lock at a time and sliding it through the straighteners. The smell of hot, freshly washed hair spreads round the room.

"It's been pretty well cut," she comments. "But there's something different about it. Where did you get it done?"

I don't tell her it was Helena; it doesn't seem like the right thing to say.

"My mum's hairdresser," I lie. "I don't know what she's called."

"Okay. But you need to get your own straighteners, your hair's too bushy," she remarks, carrying on with the job. "Actually, there's just too much of it, babe, that's what it is."

I'm getting ready for my first date.

I let Megan take charge of everything because I'm sure I'd make a mess of it on my own. I'm wearing the same dress I had on at the party; it's the only one I've got. We've added a pair of tights that Anna gave me, a bunch of black and silver bangles and a few necklaces of different lengths.

I let myself be made up again but, luckily, this time there are no hairs to be ripped out of my body.

Megan puts the straighteners down and brushes my hair, letting a lock fall over my eyes, almost covering them. I'm about to push it aside when she screams, "Are you off your head? It's taken me twenty minutes to get that right!"

I don't reply and stay very still, even though having a weird shadow over my right eye is annoying.

While Megan rummages around in her wardrobe for the perfect scarf for me, I try to summon up the strength to ask what's been bothering me since Ruben phoned.

"How d-do you think I should b-behave? Wh-what I m-mean is, I've n-never –"

"You can tell a mile off that you've never been with a boy before," she says, interrupting me. "But they usually like that, you know. Just let yourself go and it'll be all right. It's easy. Guys like to have fun, and you should want that too, right?"

The problem is, I don't really know what she means by "have fun".

"Like at the party?" I ask, unsure. I'd like to bite my nails but Megan has just painted them.

She's more or less inside the wardrobe now and her voice sounds like it's coming from behind a heavy curtain.

"Sort of. I have to say, though, you weren't exactly the life and soul of the party, were you? More like a mummified wallflower, to be honest."

She reappears with a pile of scarves and throws them on the bed beside me.

"Pick," she orders. One by one, I finger my way through the various ribbons of fabric, unsure. "The fact is, Ruben's not like other guys."

I'm suddenly alert. I want her to talk about Ruben.

"He's special, that's why. He's handsome, he studies, he's well off and he has a way with him," Megan continues, taking a scarf and laying it out in front of her to inspect it. "If you get into his crew, you're sorted."

"His crew?" I ask.

"Yes. His friends, the parties, all that stuff." She takes a scarf and wraps it round my neck several times; it's really long and fine. "This one looks perfect. Then there's the sex."

She turns away casually to get something from the desk.

The word hangs heavy in the air and it seems too big just to be here in the room with us.

"Do you understand?" Megan asks me, as I wait in troubled silence.

"N-no."

She turns round and stares at me, serious. "Did you grow up in a fairy tale?" she asks me, but I don't understand the question. "Prince Charming and all that crap?"

"I d-don't know," I admit. My gran never told me fairy tales. All she said was that I should never trust any men, especially the handsome ones. My dad was handsome.

"If you want to keep Ruben, you need to play your cards right," Megan insists. "Let go of your hang-ups and enjoy yourself. It's easy. Have fun with him."

An hour later, sitting in my bedroom waiting for Ruben to come and take me to the theatre, I mull over what Megan said.

Dread sits on my shoulders like a heavy weight. I'm filled with doubts and I think of calling him to say I'm not coming, I'm not well, I've got a temperature and can't go out with him.

Then the bell rings, cutting short my indecision. I hear my mum open the door then voices in the living room.

"Aleksandra!" she shouts. "Your friend's here."

My mum seems pleased he's come inside to introduce

himself, like in those American films where the boy comes to pick the girl up for the school prom. I hear her chatting away happily as she walks down the hall. "That's great, Aleksandra loves the theatre," she's saying in a bright voice. "And what about you, what do you do? Are you a student?"

"Yes, I'm at university, reading law."

"That'll make you the hotshot lawyer then," she says, giggling.

I step into the room and the sight of Ruben leaves me speechless. I look at him and feel like I'm floating. My heart swells up inside me because he's so gorgeous in his well-cut suit, and he's holding his hand out to me while my mum sees us off. Then I'm in the car, sitting beside the first boy I've ever gone out with in my life.

I'm so excited I can't speak, but thankfully he's turned on the stereo and has the volume up loud. It gives me time to look out the window and think, really think, that we're going to see Molière's *The Pretentious Young Ladies* in the city. Not our sleepy grey town but in a real city buzzing with bright lights, colours and life. I've never been there at night.

I went a couple of times with my gran for an afternoon doctor's appointment or when we needed to buy something we couldn't find in our town.

Ruben talks a lot on the phone as we zoom along the motorway. They're all short calls that come one after the other. Each time the phone rings, he smiles and says, "Sorry, I have to take this, it's urgent."

I don't care that he's not focusing on me. It gives me time to breathe and get used to being with him. When we sink into our red velvet seats at the theatre, our arms brushing against each other on the armrest, I can let the play carry me away and forget all my fears. I can laugh at the familiar lines and watch the professional cast bring to life a script written over three hundred and fifty years ago.

"So, did you enjoy it?" Ruben asks me, taking my hand as we leave the theatre.

"I loved it," I gush, my head still half on the stage, dazzled by the lights. "Thanks for taking me."

"Don't worry about it. We could get something to eat now then maybe stop back at my place to get to know each other better," he says, heading out to the car park. "Do you fancy that?"

"Y-yes," I reply. I fancy that. "I'm j-just w-worried about being late home," I add. "My mum will go mad and might ground me."

"Don't worry about that. I asked your mum if we could stay out a bit later tonight," he replies, driving through the brightly lit streets. "She said it was okay."

He takes me to a smart restaurant where I'm terrified I'll do something wrong. I watch him and copy what he does. I order what he orders – something with an unfamiliar name, I've no idea what – and sit up straight not resting my back on the chair, trying to smile and not let him see I'm dying of embarrassment, clueless as to how to behave.

He chats about this and that, smiling at me, taking

calls whenever his phone rings. At one point he touches my hand across the table and I feel like I'm on cloud nine again, flying high. I sip the wine he pours out for me, a red liquid I like more than the beer and the cocktails from the party. I try not to let it show, though, that I still don't like the taste much.

After dinner, we go to his house.

"This is my student flat," he explains when we go in. "Sorry about the mess. The cleaning lady doesn't come till Tuesday and I had a party last night."

It's actually quite tidy and has some nice modern furniture. Ruben puts on some music and takes a bottle out of the fridge. He opens it and signals to me to sit down with him on the sofa where he pours the contents of the bottle into two glasses.

"What should we toast?" he asks me, raising his glass.

I shrug. "I d-don't know."

"To whatever brought us together," he suggests, looking at me intensely. "What do you say?"

I know that it was my gran's death that brought us together, but I prefer to think it was Megan and our special new friendship.

Our glasses clink when they touch and I wonder if the same thing happens to people, even if you can't hear it. A silent clink that warms you inside and makes you feel like nothing bad can ever happen.

Ruben sets his glass back on the table and leans towards me.

I start to panic but at the same time feel weirdly

thrilled, as if I'm waiting for something I want with all my heart. I want to touch his face. I want to kiss his lips and run my hands through his soft hair. But I don't move. I sit stiff as a board so I don't drown in the flood of emotions surging through me.

"You're beautiful," Ruben murmurs.

He pushes my hair off my neck and starts kissing from there down along my shoulder. A shiver runs through my whole body and I close my eyes, waiting for him to kiss me on the mouth. He stays where he is, takes off my necklaces and throws them aside. He takes off the bangles too and I let him, the shivers from his mouth on my neck keeping me rooted to the spot. He nudges the neckline of my dress over, leaving more of my shoulder bare while I sit stock still. I look at the button on his shirt, the one right above his chest. I'd like to open it but I don't dare. I'm not sure it's the right thing to do.

He moves back and whispers, "Can I look at you?"

I don't know what he means so I just stare, puzzled and unable to say anything that makes any sense.

He smiles, stretches over and takes off my shoes.

Then he stands me before him, lifts up my dress and, instinctively, I try to pull it back down. But I think of Megan and what she said about boys, and I force a smile to hide my nerves.

"It's okay," he murmurs, taking hold of my dress again and pressing lightly on my hands, like a gentle caress, to encourage me to let him continue. "I just want to look at you."

I let him pull my dress over my head. The music wraps round us like a blanket, the room's dark, only the street lights filtering through the windows, and the heat from Ruben warms me like a summer sun. Stood there before him in my bra, I'd like to sink down through the floor.

Instead I let him take off my tights, slowly, so slowly.

"God, you're amazing," he says, and starts kissing my neck again.

I'm afraid he's going to touch me, I want him to touch me, I want to go home, I want to touch him. I don't move and I feel his fingers brush lightly against me.

I would never, ever have thought that being half naked in front of a boy would be so easy. This has always been something impossible for me to imagine. Never mind actually doing it, clothes dropping to the floor, eyes searching. In my head, this was always out of the question.

"Oh, you're incredible," he says in a sort of groan, leaning back to look at me. "Do you want to dance for me?" he asks.

I shake my head, unsure. It would be too difficult anyway. The embarrassment and excitement of being here with him, like this, are all tangled up, but somehow it's the only thing holding me together right now, stopping my cells from disintegrating.

He strokes my cheek. "Okay. Maybe next time. What do you want to do?"

I don't know. I don't know what you do with a boy or what he's expecting me to say.

I remember Megan's words and grab onto them like a lifebelt. "To have f-fun. W-with you."

He looks at me, his eyes so bright and so blue. I close my eyes again and wait for him to kiss me, but he sighs and plays with a lock of my hair. Then his hand slides along my neck, my shoulder blade, and stops just above my chest. "I'd like to touch you."

This must be sex. The fun Megan was talking about. Being in love with someone and wanting them to touch you, even if that's not what you want. The feeling is ripping me apart. My gran's warnings blast through my head like gusts of wind – *the world's a dangerous place for the likes of us, eyes straight ahead, don't trust boys, handsome or ugly* – and force me to say, "N-no."

I can't bear the look of disappointment on Ruben's face. He backs away a bit, just enough to deprive me of his heat, and picks up his glass to down the last few drops.

"You're right," he responds, as if deep in thought. "Maybe you're too young. Sorry."

He straightens up and I sense he's about to say he'll take me home. If that happens I know I'll never see him again. But I'm here in front of him in my bra and pants. I should enjoy the moment instead of agonising over it. I know Ruben isn't just any guy. I've never felt like this with anyone before. I have never undressed for anyone before.

My brain is going into overdrive. I want to keep Ruben. I want him to kiss me on the mouth, and maybe he will if I let him touch me. I think. And think. And think. I think about Lucy in *The Threepenny Opera*. I breathe in. I remember the lines I didn't want to say. I throw my head back and burst out laughing.

He looks at me, one eyebrow raised. I take him by the arm and pull him towards me. "Oh, it would be fun!" I exclaim, looking at him with a cheeky grin. I hope it's cheeky. "I was just acting before."

# 10

When I come out of school in the afternoon, I catch up with Megan and her mates. The thought of staying away from home as long as possible appeals to me. My mum and her husband shouldn't have to share their space with me any more than they have to. They're polite with me, the way you'd be with a guest you know is leaving soon. I always feel like it won't be long before I'm pulling my case back out from under the bed and getting ready to move again.

No one's ever said, "That's enough, it's time you left." But the fact they all tiptoe round me as if they'd rather avoid any proper contact, well, that speaks louder than words. I decide to do my homework later that night, after dinner, and to spend the afternoon like a normal teenager. Well, that's what Megan says, as we get on the bus to the shopping centre just outside of town.

We walk up and down with Anna and Kayley, checking out the sparkly window displays. When we go past the supermarket, Megan gestures to us to wait for her. She darts inside and disappears down an aisle.

We sit on a bench and wait.

Groups of boys go past and turn to look at us. They're mainly looking at Anna and Kayley, who look like they could be going to a party. They're wearing high heels, miniskirts, tight jumpers and plenty of make-up. I'm wearing jeans and a polo top under my jacket, my usual get-up, but Megan made me put lipgloss on, insisting that I can't go out without some gloss on my lips. It seems to be some sort of rule in her group so I toe the line; after all, it's not asking much.

"Him?" Anna says, lifting her chin towards one of the boys.

"Mmm," comments Kayley, crumpling her face, unsure. "Check out his jumper, it looks cheap."

Anna nods and keeps scanning the people passing by in front of us. She smiles at the boys, all of them, regardless of whether they're cute, ugly, tall or short. She even smiles at the ones who aren't boys, the older guys wandering about, mostly by themselves, who look like office workers enjoying their free time.

Megan reappears, skipping along expertly on her heels. She throws herself down on the bench beside us.

"Mission accomplished," she gloats, shaking the bag in her hand. "Shall we go into the loos?"

When we get inside, she pulls out a bottle of clear liquid, opens it, takes a swig then passes it to the others. When it gets to me, I read the label. "I d-don't r-really l-like it," I try to say, but Megan waves at me to get on with it.

"It's like medicine, Alek, you don't have to like it," she exclaims. "Take a couple of gulps and the world will seem so much nicer. And then we can go shopping too. You really need some new clothes."

I know I don't have any money and I wonder where the clothes are going to come from if my purse is empty. I take a couple of sips of the own-brand gin. It burns my throat. I can feel myself about to gag and struggle to hide it. Kayley's writing something on the mirror in lipstick and Anna's gone into a cubicle to have a pee.

"Shit," she shouts from inside. "Kayley, have you got a spare one? I've run out."

"Ruben's having a party on Saturday," Megan tells me, then takes another swig.

Kayley rummages around in her bag and throws something to Anna over the toilet door. "Thanks gorgeous," I hear her reply, then the toilet flushes.

"He told me he's invited you," Megan continues, smiling with a glazed look in her eyes. "You must have made an impression; Ruben doesn't invite just anybody to his parties."

She smiles and I blush. "B-but, I d-don't know if ..."

She puts her hands on my shoulders and looks straight at me. It's like she's staring at me but she doesn't really see me. I can smell the alcohol on her breath.

"Girl, this is your big chance. You have to come, and you absolutely have to tell us what happened between you guys the other night. That's what friends do, right, girls?"

The other two shriek in approval then reapply their lipstick.

"Megan and Anna know everything I do with boys," Kayley says, nodding her head firmly in agreement and grabbing the bottle to have another swig.

"That's because you're a hopeless tart," Anna comments, pretending to be disgusted.

"I'm not the one who went off with that bald guy at Megan's birthday," Kayley retorts. "He was so ugly I don't know how you managed not to throw up."

Anna shrugs. "I've had worse."

"Shut up, you slags," Megan shouts. "Let Aleksandra get a word in. She's the one with all the news."

Six eyes are on me now, but I really don't want to tell them what happened. It feels too private. I like going over it in my mind, thinking that it's my secret, something that makes me smile, sometimes makes me cry, something that my soul doesn't fully comprehend yet.

So that's why I turn round and go out of the toilets, with images from that night with Ruben coming back to me in flashes, one at a time. He kept his promise because he's a kind person. He looked at me and touched me, just my chest, but without undoing my bra. I was scared he wanted to take it off, but he didn't. I was so grateful I would have taken it off myself, as a gift, if I hadn't been so worried about looking silly, in a rush, babyish or bungling. I could tell he wanted to go further, he kept making groaning noises and repeating over and over, "You're incredible," but he stopped himself.

I smile as I remember.

My gran was wrong. Not all boys are bad.

Then I think about the party this Saturday, while the girls trot along behind me, giggling and staggering and calling out "Aleksandra, you bitch" in loud voices in the middle of the shopping centre. Maybe Ruben will kiss me at the next party. My first kiss will be with him and I'm looking forward to it, picturing it in my head over and over.

People are staring but they're starting to look a bit hazy to me. I can feel how strong the gin Megan made me drink is. I feel like laughing and I can hardly stand up straight. We pile onto a bench not too far from the toilets and we take a breather. We're all laughing for no reason, and a couple of boys stop and ogle us quite openly. One grins ostentatiously at Kayley.

She gets up and goes over to him. They speak for a bit, but we can't work out what they're saying because we're too far away and there's too much noise. Not long after, Kayley heads over to the Gents with the guy she's just met. I notice he's wearing low-slung jeans and a baseball cap the wrong way round.

The other two boys come over to our bench and Megan sizes them up like she's going to eat them. She crosses her legs and slides down the bench until she's practically lying down.

"All right?" they say.

"Hey," Megan replies, sounding bored.

Anna doesn't say anything. She sticks a piece of gum

in her mouth and starts chewing on it slowly. I watch, but try to scoot along to the far end of the bench because I know these two aren't here for me and I've got Ruben anyway. I don't want anyone else near me. I wait for Megan to get rid of them, she's got a boyfriend after all, but she just keeps chatting until one of them says, "We'd like to get you something. What about a Coke at the bar? Or something to eat, maybe?"

Megan shrugs. "We mean business," she tells him. "We're not here to play games."

I'm having trouble keeping up, and not just because my head's foggy from the gin. "We mean business ..." What can that mean? She's already got Lee and doesn't need a boyfriend.

"Neither are we," one of them replies.

Megan gets up at this point, says nothing but heads into the Gents toilets as well. The two boys follow her and Anna falls in behind them.

I'm left on my own. I wait.

I'm wondering why they went into the Gents and worry that one of the security guards might notice, especially when I see more men go in, some with their sons, others alone. They all come back out, though, as if nothing's happened, which means they probably didn't see the girls. I stop holding my breath but still feel uncomfortable. I don't like being here on my own.

Sitting here with my head spinning, I concentrate on thinking about Ruben until the three boys come out of the toilets and head off in different directions.

One's drying his hands on his jeans.

I jump to my feet, getting over my giddiness, and go over to look round the door.

"G-girls?" I call out. "Is ev-everything okay?"

"Wait for us outside, Alek," Megan shrills from inside. "We'll be out in a second."

They come out right after, hand in hand, looking almost like little girls. Smiling, they take my arm and cry out in unison, "Shopping time!"

I don't feel up to asking any questions. I feel a bit sick and they don't seem in the mood for chat.

We go into one shop after another. They pick up stuff from the rails, throw it at me and I catch. I try to protest because I've no idea how I'm going to pay for it all. What a mess.

"G-girls," I say loudly, exhaling so hard it comes out more like a sigh. "I d-don't have any money. I c-can't buy any of these clothes, I'm s-sorry."

Megan looks annoyed for a second then she smiles and shrugs. "We're paying. Next time it can be your turn. Okay?"

"Okay," I mumble, but I'm not convinced. Who knows when I'll be able to repay the favour. Every time my mum or her husband offer me money, I only accept the bare minimum for the school canteen or stationery. I don't want to be any more of a burden than I already am.

Megan forces me to try on some really low-cut dresses, skirts, tops, and shoes, all with heels. She chooses for me, but that's only right since it's her money. I can't say

I don't like heels, or that I feel ashamed in this red dress that hardly covers my chest, or that a jumper that leaves half your tummy exposed isn't much of a jumper to me.

I feel like her plaything, her doll again, and she seems so happy I don't want to disappoint her.

"These will be perfect for the party," she concludes, teaming a skirt with a top. "And keep these other ones as spares, for another night. It's a pain none of us can lend you anything, but your boobs are too big."

The next stop is a lingerie shop where she has me try on bra-and-pants sets in black lace, white and cream. I don't like the lace, but the girls assure me it looks amazing and that the next time I'm with Ruben I'll knock him for six just by undressing down to my underwear.

I'd like some normal pants, but Megan shakes her head.

"Thong. Has to be, nothing else will do," she states, bursting out laughing. She grabs my old skin-tone support bra and matching pants and throws them into the bin near the till.

"You won't be needing those any more," she tells me. She hugs me affectionately in the changing room, even though I'm half naked, and she whispers in my ear, "You're gorgeous, Alek. You really are."

Before I put my clothes back on, I look in the mirror. I don't recognise the girl looking back.

She has perfect, shoulder-length straight hair and lipgloss that makes her mouth glisten like a ripe cherry. She's wearing black lace pants that barely cover her crotch, and a matching bra that pushes up her breasts so they stay up high instead of being flattened.

I let Ruben and Megan's words sink in.

I'm incredible. I'm gorgeous, beautiful, amazing. I'm a star.

The sense of embarrassment stays with me, though, as I realise these clothes aren't mine. But the euphoric feeling of looking like a woman is so hard to resist. It's hypnotic. I look like a woman even though I'm not really old enough to be one yet, and I can't stop worrying about getting things wrong. But this is the most important role of my life; I don't want to mess it up. I want to become the part, to be perfect and play it without being scared of what people will think, like I do in the theatre. This time, though, there'll be only one spectator to applaud, or get up and leave the room before the performance is over.

We get the bus home and the giddy effect of the gin wears off. Anna and Kayley fall asleep against each other and we have to wake them up when we get to their stop.

Megan and I walk down our street but she has to stop and throw up in a bush. I don't feel too well either but I didn't drink as much as the other three so it's not as bad.

When I get home, I lock eyes with my mum for a second as she turns round to say hello from the kitchen and I realise I've got all these shopping bags with me.

"Alek," she says, concerned. "I tried to phone you. Where have you been all this time?"

"At th-the shop-p-ping centre with M-Megan and the others," I reply, unable to move. I'm standing in the doorway as if I'm expecting to be thrown out for being late, because I smell of alcohol or because it's ten o'clock and I haven't done my homework yet.

My mum keeps staring at me but doesn't seem to know what to say.

"Where did you get all those bags?" she finally asks.

"I b-bought some c-clothes," I reply, grappling for a plausible way of explaining the money I spent, which I shouldn't have had in the first place. "I h-had some m-money saved up. Gran g-gave it me."

She turns back to pull something out of the oven. A plate covered in tinfoil. She puts it on the table, still set for dinner, in the place that's now mine.

"I kept your dinner warm," she says.

"Th-thanks."

I'm absolutely starving so I wolf down the stew in a couple of forkfuls. My mum is on the other side of the table, checking some notes on printed sheets full of annotations that she keeps adding to.

As soon as I've finished, I get up to go and do my homework, putting my plate in the dishwasher.

My mum's voice startles me. "Is everything all right, Aleksandra?"

"Of c-course," I stammer, attempting a smile and walking away before she can say anything else. I don't know how much longer I'll be able to keep it up if she asks me any more questions.

In my room, I sit down at the desk and open my books.

The words move in and out of focus, all muddled up. I try to concentrate but my head's high in the clouds yet heavy at the same time. My stomach lurches, churning up the stew with what's left of the gin.

I need to lie down.

I lie on the bed, fully dressed, and before I know it, I'm fast asleep.

# 11

Maybe it's not what I thought I saw. I'm at Ruben's party and the lighting's dim, but on the other side of the half-closed door to Ruben's bedroom, not too far from me, I thought I saw Lee slap Megan.

I scan the room looking for Ruben, but there are too many people and when I eventually spot him, he's caught up in a heated debate with a bunch of guys. The music is really loud but it doesn't seem to bother anyone, and the neighbours aren't complaining. The glass that Anna thrust at me as soon as we got here is empty now. I stick it behind a plant, and move over to the door. A finger of light is filtering out.

"I want more," I hear Lee bark. "Is that clear?"

Then nothing, just an unnerving silence.

I wait for him to say something else, but the words fill the room as if there was nothing else to say. He wants more. Maybe Megan doesn't love him. I don't really understand how she can go out with someone like Lee anyway. He doesn't speak to anyone, never laughs, and he isn't kind like Ruben.

I'm about to open the door to check Megan's all right when he barges past, pushing me aside. "Get out the way, slag," he hisses and I'm shocked because he's never spoken to me before. Those are the first words he's ever said to me.

I see him furrow through the hordes, too tall and heavy-set to cross the room without leaving a trail behind him. Megan comes out right after him, smiling. She's started dancing already and she takes my hand to drag me back to the party.

"I-is everything o-okay?" I ask her.

"Of course," she exclaims, a bit too enthusiastically. "He gets a bit crazy every now and then, but it doesn't last. It's the garage you know, he set it up on his own and now he's got money problems."

We get to the table being used as a bar where she nervously sloshes out a cocktail for me and shouts, "Cheers!"

She adds more vodka, a lot more, to our glasses, and winks at me.

"D-did he just h-hit you?" I insist, still a bit wary. It looks like her lip's trembling, even though she's trying to hide it.

"Don't be daft," she replies, insulted. "You're seeing things, you're drunk already. Get a bit more drunk and forget about it."

We drink, and while I hold my breath so I don't have to taste it, praying the burning sensation in my throat will pass, we see Anna, Kayley and Dani stand up on the sofa and start dancing.

Megan shrieks, slams her glass down and rushes over to them, leaping onto the cushions in her heels. She yanks off her top as if she were suddenly feeling far too hot, and stands there in her bra, and the others do the same, throwing their tops at the boys who've formed a ring around them.

They're standing in my way, so I can't see what's happening, but I'm not moving from here because I'm afraid they'll insist I join in. The skirt I'm wearing is really short and tight, I honestly don't think I could move in it.

"Your friends are wild," Ruben says, appearing by my side. He leans on the window ledge beside me, brushing his arm against mine. "Do you not feel like dancing too?"

I shake my head and a wave of vodka-induced dizziness comes over me. It makes me want to giggle, so I do, because Ruben is beside me for the first time since I got to his house for the party, and I don't know what else to do.

"Dance with me, go on," he urges.

I let him put his hands on my hips and we move together, almost touching. My skirt rides up but I don't dare pull it down because Ruben's hands are resting on it and I don't want him to move them.

"I like how you move," he comments, pulling himself closer. I smell his scent again. The dizziness from the drink quickens, and all of a sudden I'm on a merry-go-round bobbing through the sky, rising and falling to the music and laughter. I am the music. I am the laughter.

And I want Ruben to kiss me.

He kisses my neck, still dancing, and nudges my top over to leave my shoulder bare. A pleasant heat surges through my body. I cling to him and close my eyes, every now and then opening them to flashes of what's happening on the sofa. Megan and the others are now in their bras and pants, dancing with the guys who are hanging on their every move. Ruben slips his hand inside my top and whispers in my ear, "Please."

I feel like laughing again. I realise there are people right next to us but I don't want to pull away from Ruben, I can't risk him leaving me like the other night, even though I'd rather he didn't touch me in front of all these people. I cling to him and my vision blurs, the beat of the music gets heavier and heavier, his hands sweep over me, his breath in my ear. Megan's taken her bra off now too. One minute I feel like I'm sinking, the next I'm floating, his hands moving over me again, mine tight round his neck, this guy who might not be mine, although I wish he was.

"Come with me," he murmurs, speaking into my ear so I can hear him over the music, which is beating as fast as my heart and hammering in my head. I stagger along behind him without stopping to straighten my clothes because no one's bothered, least of all me. Everyone else is dancing and drinking. I've no idea where I am. I don't even know if my feet are touching the ground or not. The ceiling has switched places with the floor, I'm sure of it, and my stomach's churning, trying to switch places with my heart. I fight the nausea because I like this blurry feeling I'm flying on. Everyone's having fun. I'm having fun. I go into Ruben's bedroom. He doesn't shut the door and pushes me gently onto the bed. Or maybe I fall because I can't stand up. I don't want to have sex, I tell myself as I let him take my top off. I don't know this guy at all. I don't know myself. The room's spinning.

"I just want to look at you," he says over and over. He unzips his trousers, probing my face with a penetrating gaze, as if seeking to explain what he says next. "Do you mind?"

I don't have the foggiest, faintest clue what it is that I might mind. All I can hear is the music and my heart beating faster and faster. I feel like laughing, and crying too.

He presumes I mean no and reaches down into his boxers. His blue eyes stare at me intently and, as he touches himself, he moans. I feel his gaze slide down onto my breasts. His eyes devour them, the rhythmic movement of his hand seeming to keep time with the music. Behind him I catch sight of the door, almost wide open, but I try to ignore it. In my complete inability to work out what's going on, the one thing I do understand is that if I move from here, I'll be making a big mistake.

I'm lying on a bed in my bra and a skirt no wider than a belt while Ruben touches himself, and I feel like the thickest, most boring person in the whole universe. I should be doing something. I know I should be doing something instead of lying here like a zombie. The thought that, afterwards, he'll think I'm a complete idiot torments me. He keeps touching himself, then he says, "Take it off." I feel the vodka in my throat, my vision blurs, and I unhook my bra.

I throw it to the side and rest on my elbows, my breasts bare, my skin burning under Ruben's searing gaze.

"You drive me wild. You drive me wild," he repeats over and over, then sort of shudders, leans forward and groans for a second. He lays his head on my stomach and I feel his silky hair tickle me. I caress his neck until he gets up and does up his trousers. He looks shaken. "I'm just going to the bathroom, I won't be long."

I wait for him on the bed and try to cover myself up with movements that don't seem like my own, as if I were watching from above. The fog in my head lifts a little now I'm on my own, and I wonder what's just happened between me and Ruben. I'm scared. But I feel free too. I want to get out of here, now. I wish he'd come back and hold me. Kiss me. Then, all of a sudden, I feel lost and a sense of guilt tears through me like a burning flame. All my gran's warnings echo round my head. I'd die of shame if she could see me now.

Yet, part of the warm feeling inside comes from somewhere else, and it's different from shame. It's something intimate and I wish Ruben were here to talk to about it. Maybe tomorrow, when the party's finished. Or I could talk to Megan and ask her if what we've just done means we're together now. Me and him.

I like the sound of it. Me and him.

No more Aleksandra on her own.

I lie back and close my eyes. The bed sways beneath me, who knows where it'll take me. When I open my eyes again, I've no idea how long they've been closed. I must've fallen asleep. I get up and try to walk straight, aiming for the bathroom to look for Ruben. I push the door and it opens.

Without switching on the light, I go over to the toilet, suddenly realising that I've come in to be sick. I bend over and retch repeatedly.

My head throbs and it feels like I'm on the point of a heart attack. I'd like to call out for help but I haven't got the energy to scream and the music's so loud that no one would hear me anyway. There's a constant hissing noise in my ears but, just below it, I hear something else too. A moan. I get up and dry my mouth on a piece of toilet paper. I turn round to go back into the bedroom, and it's only then that I notice something behind the door, by the bath. A guy sitting on the edge, a girl with her head between his legs. From her hair, it looks like Dani but I'm not sure; she's hardly got any clothes on. The guy stares at me and smiles as if my being there, in the dark, watching them doing whatever it is they're doing, is completely normal.

I rush out, going over on my heels on the tiles, and seek refuge in the living room. The girls aren't on the sofa any more, they've put their clothes back on and a lot of the guests have gone. Only Lee and a couple of Ruben's friends are still there.

"There you are," exclaims Ruben when he sees me. He

comes towards me and puts his arm on my shoulders. We sit down and I catch my breath because getting here from the bathroom was a bit of a struggle. Out of the corner of my eye, I see the guy who was sitting on the bath slipping out the front door, waving over to us as he leaves.

"You were sleeping earlier. I didn't want to wake you. Are you okay? You must've drunk too much vodka," Ruben says. He moves closer and whispers, "You make me behave like an idiot. Sorry for earlier."

I don't know what to say, so I wait for him to say something else and enjoy just being near him. He pushes my hair off my face and adds, "We hardly know each other, I know. But I really don't know what comes over me when I see you. I can't stop myself. You're so exciting. So beautiful."

I can see my cleavage easily from here, I only have to tilt my head forward a few degrees. Exciting. He's right. Maybe that explains the shirts and polo tops two sizes too big.

"Didn't you realise you have this effect on men?" Ruben asks me, running his finger under my chin. "It's a gift."

No, I didn't realise. But my gran clearly did, that's why she tried to hide me. But from what? My brain is whirling in reverse, trying to turn back time and piece the fragments together. Hiding does make sense sometimes. But what harm is there in giving a boy something more? Is it wrong to be in love, to want to get to know each other?

For Megan, Anna, Kayley and Dani, and all the other girls at the party tonight, it's like a game. They laugh, they're happy, they don't take themselves seriously, they don't stutter, they don't hammer furiously, and they don't skulk among the broken spotlights of an ancient theatre, like the people I've been spending my time with until now.

"You might feel it's wrong," Ruben continues. "But we're young, it's our time to have fun. Don't you think?"

I nod. Dani comes into the living room, looking a bit dazed. I'd like to talk to her, but Ruben squeezes me so I don't.

"You were great. And if there's anything you don't want to do, just tell me," he says. "At first I thought you were a bit young for us, you know. Even if you're the same age as Megan you don't seem, well, you don't seem like you've had much experience."

I go red and I'm grateful it's dark. He's going to say it now. He's going to say I'm pathetic and did something wrong back there in the bedroom. I feel the disappointment push me to tears and I grip the cushions on the sofa.

"But you were amazing tonight," he says, making my heart explode with something I've never felt before. Pride? Relief? Whatever it is, it's all mixed up with my feelings for Ruben, which are multiplying at lightning speed. "You're a real woman, Aleksandra, I was wrong."

I don't get the chance to reply because the doorbell goes and Anna goes over to open it, smiling as if she were expecting someone. There's a boy standing on the doorstep with a stack of pizza boxes.

"Are you hungry?" Ruben asks me, getting up. "We ordered something to eat while you were sleeping."

A minute later we're all sitting round the table wolfing down slices of hot pizza. Megan is sitting in Lee's lap and he seems a bit less surly than usual. We drink ice-cold Coke that clears our heads after the vodka, and as the alcohol-induced fog starts to lift, we chat about the next party and the things we'd like to do this summer, or when we're older. They're all just pipe dreams, but it's fun to share them. Megan wants to go to a catwalk show in Paris and sit with the VIPs wearing one of her own dresses, waiting for people to come over to her and say, "What a gorgeous dress! Is it Valentino? No. Armani? No. Really? Are you sure?" And she'll answer, "Of course I'm sure, I designed it myself and made it with my own two hands."

It's a lovely dream. Maybe it's the one she wished for at her birthday party, when she blew out the candles.

Anna and Kayley want to go to Las Vegas, win a fortune, then come home and become famous singers. They improvise a song together and I get goose bumps because they're so good, their voices glowing like candles in a darkened room.

Dani wants to swim with dolphins, and Lee wants to watch a MotoGP world championship in Indianapolis.

"Why Indianapolis?" Ruben asks.

Lee shrugs and replies, "Dunno, just sounds good."

We all laugh. Then Megan asks, "What about you, Alek? What would you like to do?"

I think about it. No one's ever asked me before, I haven't even asked myself. The answer comes quick and certain but I only realise it as I'm saying the words. "I w-wish my th-theatre group d-didn't have to shut down. I wish I h-h-had enough m-money to save it."

"You act?" Lee exclaims, bursting out laughing, really loud. "And h-how the f-fuck do you d-d-d-do that?"

The others laugh too, but this time I try not to get upset. I shrug it off and bite into my pizza, feeling like I'm part of the group, the only group I'll have left in a few months. I like being here in the middle of the night, with Ruben, his hand resting on my leg.

# 12

"What are you doing?"

"I'm s-sleeping."

"Don't you want to play?"

"N-no."

"Why not?"

"Because I've g-got a sore head."

There's silence for a second. I feel someone climbing onto the bed beside me, plonking himself more or less on my stomach. I push Matt away with my hand, forcing him against the wall, but he doesn't seem to mind, and stays there. He's singing. I sigh. I can't keep him away from me. There's no key in the door and I don't want to ask my mum if there is one somewhere. I can't say to her, "I want to keep your brat out."

"Is your head broken?"

"No. It j-just h-hurts."

"Why?"

I don't answer. He asks too many questions. Whatever you answer, he's never happy, and right away he hits you with another one. I don't know how he does it. Why,

why, why, it's like a singsong, and sometimes he doesn't even seem to care what you reply, he just likes the sound of the word.

Like the word *daddy*. Maybe it's the three *d*s that he likes.

"Do you want to play Hungry Hippos?"

"N-no."

"You're not to eat all the balls though," he explains, in a tone he's obviously picked up from our mum. *Our mum* pops into my head the minute I think it. "Only the hippo can eat the balls. Or we could play the pirate game. The pirate with the swords. If you poke him he pops up and looks for the treasure, but you can't see him ..."

He launches into a nonsensical monologue, a complicated story with no apparent meaning about a plastic pirate. Last time, the main character was a potty shaped like a huge ladybird.

"... it buzzes then it runs and jumps and pulls out the sword then swoosh and boom and the cannon fires."

My phone rings on the desk. I get up and leave Matt to his imaginary world. Ruben's name flashes on the screen and I immediately stop to think if I should answer or not. I stutter more on the phone, especially when it's him.

I imagine I'm Hester in the play. I take a deep breath.

"Hello?"

"Hi, I hope I'm not interrupting anything?" he says. I can hear car engines and a car radio in the background.

"No, you're not," I reply.

"If you're not busy, do you want to come out with me?

I'm going for a sunbed session at my friend's salon," he explains.

I haven't done my homework.

I've got a sore head.

I wouldn't have the faintest idea what to do in a tanning salon. And I've got rehearsals at the theatre in a few hours.

"Okay," I reply, excited already at the prospect of seeing him again. We haven't seen each other since the party on Saturday. He's been busy studying, he tells me, but I miss him, so all the rest can wait.

"I'll be over in two minutes."

In the time it takes me to run a comb through my hair, he's pulling up in front of the house.

I go into the kitchen to see my mum, my jacket on already. "Do you mind if I go out with Ruben?" I ask her, picking up my keys.

"No," she replies, without looking up from the laptop she's always busy at. "Don't be late though, you've got school tomorrow."

I'm about to go out the front door when she calls me back. "Would you pick up some bread for dinner?"

I take the money she gives me and finally I'm outside in Ruben's car. He's wearing a cream polo neck and a brown leather jacket, and he smiles at me before we drive away.

"I've got a surprise for you," he says. "I was hoping you'd be free."

"Wh-what is it?" I ask. I'm not keen on surprises and

I'm hoping tanning's not involved, because I don't think I'd like it.

"Wait and see," he says, with a cute smile.

We get to his friend's beauty salon, and he wasn't joking – he really does have a sunbed booked. Then he says, "While I'm through there, Lisa will take care of you. I've asked her to treat you like a princess." He brushes my cheek with his finger. "Have fun."

Minutes later I'm at the mercy of this Lisa, a beautician and hairdresser with over-tinted hair, who smells of vanilla, or maybe honey. She prattles on non-stop, recounting gossip about clients of the salon or TV and film celebrities. She's very well-informed, and quick. She has me sit on a padded swivel chair and announces, "We'll start with your head, okay? That means I can do your nails while we're waiting on the dye."

I'd like to be with Ruben, not with her.

And I've no idea what it means to be treated like a princess. Lisa washes my hair, then cuts it doing some weird things with the scissors – "To thin it down a bit," she tells me – and plasters on a cream that stinks and makes my head itch so much I think it might be acid. Then she gets a pair of tweezers and plucks my eyebrows. I squirm in the chair, my eyes watering with the pain, but she just keeps saying over and over, "We're nearly done. I'm redrawing your brow line to accentuate your eyes and cheekbones. Just wait and see."

The way she says "wait and see", you'd think I was about to discover something amazing, when all I want is for Ruben to hurry up so we can get out of here.

Then I notice the other women in the salon, all getting the same things done as me. They're chilled out, flicking through magazines and chatting with the salon girls. The background music is catchy and the posters on the walls show gorgeous girls with perfect skin and shiny hair. It strikes me that maybe that's the way Ruben wants me, that Lisa's job is to improve me. I look in the mirror and a worried face looks back at me.

I have shadows under my eyes because I've been staying up late, trying to keep up with my homework before I slump into bed. I don't have time in the afternoons because I spend them at Megan's or hanging out with her and the others, when I'm not rehearsing at the theatre.

My polo top's hanging off my shoulders like a badly hung curtain. It's faded and nondescript. Just like my pale, dull skin and my boring face. I'm not perfect like the poster girls, or even like the other women sitting in the salon. I'm not like them, I'm not like them, I'm not like them. I start to panic, then tell myself that I'm in the right place, so it'll all be okay. Ruben has more experience and knows what I need. I just have to let things take their course and I'll feel less confused, less inadequate.

I hope and pray, crossing my legs and trying to relax like the others, while Lisa files my nails.

"What colour do you want?" she asks, pulling out a box full of nail polishes.

"I don't know," I reply, taking a look at them.

"What do you think of the pewter? It's totally on

point, but it's a bit moody," she says, extracting a bottle. "I've got a more shimmery version as well."

The girl in the poster beside the mirror has pearly white nail polish on. "I like that." I point, shyly.

"We normally use that for brides, but who cares," Lisa says. "Let's use the silvery one to soften the wedding effect, what do you think?"

"Okay," I mumble, finding it impossible to cope with this conversation.

The rest of the time, I look on as my image gradually changes in front of my eyes. My curly, wild auburn hair is now jet black and perfectly smooth.

"It'll last a couple of months," Lisa tells me, "then you'll have to have the straightening treatment again."

My face is all made up, shiny; my eyes are wider, my mouth softer.

Lisa explains how to apply it myself and gives me a make-up case with powder, foundation, lipsticks, eye- and lip-liners and eyeshadows. "A present from Ruben," she says, winking at me.

When I get out I'm in a daze.

I'm so happy with this new face I've got that I throw myself into Ruben's arms as soon as I see him, and I have to stop myself from doing a twirl like Megan would. It's like a first night at the theatre, when I'm in my stage clothes and Electra does my make-up and hair for the part. Only this time, I won't have to put my boring Aleksandra face back on. I can go on enjoying the thrill of not being me. Ruben showers me with compliments and squeezes my hand before we get back into the car. I lean over to kiss him, feeling bold and wanting to taste his lips, just once. But his phone rings and he smiles at me, indicating that he has to take the call. It's urgent. So I straighten up, sigh and pull down the vanity mirror to look at my perfect eyes.

My afternoon as a princess isn't over. We go shopping next. When we stop in the car park of a shopping centre, I admit to Ruben that I don't have any money. He tells me not to worry, that it's a present, and maybe one day I'll give him a present too. That's the way it is between boys and girls, isn't it? I nod and let him buy me jumpers, jeans, shoes, T-shirts and thousands of other things that he picks out personally. The shoes all have high heels but I decide not to protest, even though the trainers I wear for gym at school are falling apart and I still won't ask my mum for a new pair.

"There's a party tonight. Do you want to come?" he asks me when we get back in the car, after taking another couple of calls on his mobile. "Megan will be there. Lee and I can come and pick you up at ten, if that's okay."

I can't go out at ten, my mum would never let me – it's Thursday today. But the idea of missing out on a night out with my friend and my boyfriend takes the edge right off my good mood.

"If you can't, it doesn't matter," he says, breaking my pained silence. "But we won't be able to see each other this weekend. I'm going on a ski trip with my parents."

"N-no, of c-course I c-can," I reply, my heart hammering and my ears burning. "I'll s-see you at t-ten."

"That's great," he says, as he lets me out in front of the theatre. I stop for a second, he's looking straight at me and I think he wants to kiss me, now. But we're interrupted by his phone ringing so I give him a feeble wave, pick up my bags and get out of the car.

He races off and I'm left in a parallel world that smells of dust and musty old fabric. It's a world that's not new to me, only it hasn't yet seen the new Aleksandra, and when someone does something normal, like trying to get off the Ship of Fools, this world becomes alarmed.

"What on earth have you done to yourself?" Electra says, inspecting my face as if trying to see inside my head. "Did your mother let you out like that? You're late and you're hardly going to be believable now as Hester."

I feel like dying. My eyes fill with tears. Ever since I joined this group, they've been telling me to be myself, but now that I am, they criticise me. Thomas is the only one who tries to be kind.

"Come on, Electra! She can wear a wig for the play," he tells her. "She looks fine the way she is."

Electra doesn't say anything else and turns round to go back on stage. From his mixing desk, Jonah shakes his head and looks at me as if I were a rare species. "You don't look like you," he says.

This hurts me, I don't know why. He's always teased me for my flannel shirts and my hair which goes frizzy when I'm anywhere near water, so why isn't he encouraging me? Then I remember that Jonah doesn't

120

encourage anyone – all he knows how to do is belittle, so I try not to let it bother me.

The real problem, the big, inexplicable one, is the hammering.

Helena is practically smashing the scenery to bits. She's hammering so violently it's like she's knocking down the theatre.

"Oh dear. I don't think our set designer approves of your new look," Jonah says, laughing. "Maybe it's because you trashed the haircut she gave you?"

"Give it a break," I exclaim, furious all of a sudden. "I couldn't care less what you lot think. You're just a bunch of losers."

Jonah looks at me. He doesn't smirk, he does something much worse. He frowns. It's as if he doesn't recognise me, and his eyes cloud over with something I often see in people who have anything to do with me. It's the shadow of disappointment.

I feel hurt by this too, but even worse, it scares me. Jonah's never disappointed, he's too busy joking around, playing the madman in the rafters, making my life impossible with his sarky comments. I can't disappoint him if he doesn't expect anything from me. He always treats me like I'm good for nothing, throwing water at me, insulting me.

But this, I can't stand this.

How dare he be let down, he doesn't even know me! I've been here for three years and he's never once asked me why I joined the group, or rather, what my problem is. It's obvious; he doesn't care about other people's problems. He doesn't care about anyone apart from himself, which is why that look on his face makes my blood boil.

"L-loser," I repeat, trembling with rage and taking a step nearer.

He puts his hands over his crotch. "If you get any closer, I swear I'll bite you," he warns me, gesturing with his chin. "How about trying to calm her down instead? Clown face."

He's right. I decide to ignore the umpteenth insult from him and set off into the wings, tottering on my heels to find Helena where she works at the back corner of the stage.

"Quack quack," Jonah taunts me from behind. "That's some waddle you've got there, Lady Hester."

I ignore him; Helena's freaking out and, out of the corner of my eye, I see Thomas and Electra talking in low voices about how to calm her down while the rest of the group stand stock still, like they're listening, ready to jump into action if the racket turns into something more dangerous.

When I get nearer, she stops banging and points her hammer at me, fire in her eyes.

"What's wrong, Helena?" I ask her gently. "Is it my fault?"

She nods and bangs her hammer on the floor with all her might. It bounces up again and I have to stop myself from running away. Thomas should be dealing with this fit of hers, but I can't pull out now, since I'm the one she's angry with.

"It's j-just h-hair dye," I try to explain. "To l-look prettier."

She bangs again, sharply, which is her way of saying, *bullshit*. Yet again, I marvel at the depth of emotion that can be expressed with a hammer.

"My h-hair will go b-back the w-way it was," I say. Her beautiful, bright green eyes glare at me in disgust, but I falter on. "It's j-just that ... I've g-got a b-boyfriend now. You c-can't go out with a b-boyfriend l-l-looking like a s-sack of p-potatoes."

Helena grips the hammer as if she'd like to throw it at me. She looks me up and down and stops to take in not just my hair, but also my low-cut skinny jumper, my tight jeans that are as slim-fitting as the label says, swathing my hips, and my high heels peeking out at the end of the skin-tight legs.

Then she gets up and hurls the hammer with the full force of both her arms. She hurls it as far as she can, and it flies towards the bathroom door. The pane of glass in the top half smashes into a thousand pieces.

But no one worries about that. The glass makes a smash, but it startles us less than the sound coming out of Helena's mouth. A roar. *"Aaaahhh,"* she yelled as she threw the hammer, like a tennis player reaching out for a big serve and grunting with effort.

We all stand frozen to the spot.

Helena starts crying and Thomas hurries away to call

her mum because she's out of control and no one knows how to handle her. Helena has never done anything violent before. We've never heard her scream before. Hearing her voice is a shock, like whiplash, and it leaves us rooted to the spot. I provoked that scream, and I've no idea how. When I go over to ask her, she tries to grab my hair and I jump out of the way just in time. Electra suggests I keep out of the way and goes over to her, staying at a safe distance because Helena still has her tool belt on.

"Crikey, clown face," says Jonah from just behind me. "Your new look is a bit of a scream, as they say."

I don't laugh.

I think back to the day I didn't go to school and what Electra and Thomas said about Helena and the terrible thing that had happened to her. This must all have something to do with me, my face, my clothes ... who knows, but it unnerves me more than I'd have thought possible.

I'm happy when Thomas tells us to go home, that rehearsals have been suspended. I leave the theatre behind Jonah who's fiddling with something, which he then throws onto the pavement as soon we get out.

"Later," he says and heads off as if he doesn't have anywhere to go.

I'm about to walk to the bus stop when I notice the thing that Jonah tossed on the ground. I bend down to pick it up, and just when I'm thinking his bad manners know no bounds, I recognise it. It's the same as the piece of plastic that fell on the stage the day of my monologue. The time when I lost my concentration and got stuck on the last lines.

I vow to make him pay, sooner or later, for what he puts me through, but right now I'm so angry I'd like a hammer of my own to hurl at him, to smash him into tiny pieces. Then I'd throw them all in the bin.

I think about that all the way home and the bags of shopping slip my mind until I'm nearly at the gate. I've got far too many bags this time, all filled with flashy designer gear. I don't want my mum seeing them and finding out that Ruben has bought me so many presents. My instinct tells me that she'll ask questions I don't feel like answering.

So I slip into the garden beside the garage and sneak down the side of the house, like I've been doing it all my life, crouching so no one will see me. I sit the bags below my bedroom window then go back the way I came, hurrying into the house and hoping to get in without being seen.

But my new look is destined to attract attention, including that of my mum and her husband. They gaze at me in silence for a few seconds then turn to each other, as if to decide what their joint reaction should be.

"Alek, what a difference!" my mum exclaims, feigning enthusiasm. The veil of concern on her face doesn't bother me. I've got too much adrenaline surging through my veins after the events of this afternoon and the prospect of the evening ahead. I just want to have a shower to calm down. "Do you want to tell me where you've been and how you paid for everything you've clearly had done?"

Her husband doesn't take his eyes off me, and I wish he'd disappear before he gets any big ideas about coming over all fatherly with me. He looks just like he's about to speak to me.

"Ruben treated me," I say before he has chance to speak.

"Okay," my mum says, slowly. "I spoke to Carla about him and she said he comes from a good family and that he's really bright. So, I don't mind you going out with him."

Fine. I'm about to go to my room when my mum takes a breath. She's working herself up to say something else; I can sense it, so I wait.

"But maybe you should take it one step at a time, don't you think?" she continues. "Accepting lots of gifts, so early on and for no reason, might give him the wrong idea."

"What do you mean?" I ask, confused.

"I mean, he might think you want to get serious with him," she says, letting out a sigh. I can tell she finds it difficult, talking about this stuff with me. I'm feeling uneasy too. I'm getting lessons in love from the woman who got herself pregnant by a boy she met at a party when she was eighteen. "Get to know him better before you give him so much space in your life."

I'd like to say, "But I want to get serious with him. And I want to give him every inch of my life." I'd also like to ask her permission to go to the party but I'm so certain she'll refuse that I don't. All I do is nod, and say, "Okay."

She stares at me a bit longer. "Okay, then," she concludes. "Did you get the bread I asked you to buy?"

"No. I'm sorry, I forgot."

I'm surprised that I don't even sound sorry. My voice is cold and distant, as if it's undergone some kind of treatment too.

"It doesn't matter, I've got some in the freezer," she tells me, and I take this to mean I can go. My mum and her husband go back to watching television. I slip into the hall, my head in turmoil as I try to think of a way of going to the party with Ruben and the others.

I shut my bedroom door, open the window wide and lean out to get my bags.

I stop for a second to look at the dark open space where the window was and I realise that getting in and out of the house whenever I want isn't going to be such a problem after all.

# 13

I wait for my mum to put Matt to bed and shut herself
up in her bedroom with her husband, like she does every
night.

I wait for the house to go quiet before I get up
and rummage through the bags under my bed to find
something to wear. For the first time ever, I take my time
getting ready, looking at the clothes and imagining what
I'll look like in them.

I put on the matching thong and lacy bra, my heart
racing for no reason.

I choose a low-cut dress with a short skirt, but I don't
put tights on because I've noticed that Megan and the
others never wear any. I climb into my new heels, a pair of
silver stiletto sandals, and tip my head upside down for a
few seconds, run my fingers through my hair and then pat
it down to tidy it up. The girl in the mirror takes my breath
away. Sophisticated and sexy, very sure of herself. Me.

That's me. That's me.

I have to say it over and over in my head to believe it,
and even while I'm smiling at my reflection, I can hardly

take it in. I'm somewhere inside this much better version of me.

I'm in the car now, sitting in the back seat beside Megan, who's looking beautiful and surly, and has a bluish-green mark on her shoulder. She's talking incessantly, telling me how it's going to be a real party this time because some older guys that go to university with Ruben are coming. It's going to be a big night for us.

I don't ask her how she got the bruise and I don't really listen to her either, because as soon as I got in we had a swig of peach vodka and I feel like I'm starting to float. I can't concentrate on anything but the back of Ruben's neck in front of me.

I just want to get to the party quickly so I can be with him, dance with him, hold him, kiss him. I thought I might try again. Maybe he's waiting for me to make a move because he'd rather follow my lead, when I feel ready to get serious. That's why I've decided I'm going to kiss him tonight.

Excited at the thought, I hurry into the house where the party's being held, practically skipping behind Megan. I can't stop laughing and I gulp down the cocktail Ruben gives me with a knowing wink. I can read so many things in his eyes, one of which is a promise for me. We'll be together tonight; we'll find a quiet corner just for us before he goes away on his ski trip.

"Hey, Alek, I think we're going to be the main attraction," Megan exclaims, looking around the living room of the house. It's packed full of university students, but there are also girls from our school. I see Dani chatting to a couple of guys and maybe Kayley and Anna are around somewhere too.

Megan's comment alerts me to the fact that a lot of people are looking at us. We're leaning on the drinks table next to each other, and we must be making quite an impression. Megan, slim, blonde, the free spirit. Me with my ink-black hair and voluptuous curves, a wary look in my eyes. She takes my hand and squeezes it, as if we're a team, and says, "Come on, let's give them a better look."

We walk across the room together, from corner to corner, as if we're going somewhere or looking for someone, hand in hand, swaying our hips and laughing at something funny, although we don't really know what. Euphoria. Excitement. No one can take this part from us – we're centre-stage, playing the lead in our fantastic costumes. We have the best-looking guys at the party. No one has Ruben's class, his sparkly blue eyes or kind heart. I feel so lucky and so very happy. I'm a part of something, at the centre of a life free of pain, no more shadows of the past, no more impenetrable rules and dark days spent on my own playing the invisible girl.

A guy comes over to us, quite cute but short, and says to Megan, "If you show me your tits, I'll give you twenty."

He's smiling and at ease, which throws me for a second. I'm sure I heard him properly, but it's such an outrageous request that Megan and I burst out laughing, propping each other up.

Then she straightens up, looks at him defiantly and holds out a hand. He places a £20 note on it – he had it ready, as if he knew what the answer would be. I hold my breath; I can't believe Megan has actually accepted. Then, while my head spins and the world goes more and more out of focus, I see her lift up her top, slowly and calculatingly. She holds it half way up for a second, the curve of her breasts just visible. The boy in front of us feigns a heart attack and reaches out to help her. She pulls back and shakes her head like she's dealing with a naughty little boy. "Oh, no," she says. "Twenty buys a look, not a feel."

She dances around, swaying her hips and lifting her top right up until her chest is in full view. She's standing there as natural as anything, and no one honestly seems to have noticed. Apart from the boy, who looks like he wants to do more than look.

"How much do you want for a feel?" he asks. Megan has a think about it and I look on, gawping, fascinated and dazzled like a deer caught in a car's headlights.

"Maybe later," she says. "There's a queue, you know. What makes you think you're so special?"

We laugh. The boy nods and slopes off, but I see him every now and then, turning towards us to eye Megan up. She ignores him and smiles at me.

"See how easy it is?" she says. "They're just jerks – they'd do anything to cop a pair of tits."

She looks at me, waiting for a reply, but I'm too flabbergasted to say anything. This is all new to me, but I don't think it can be wrong if no one seems bothered by what Megan and the others do. And all that boy did was look. Maybe it's a game, like when they threw the cream around at Megan's party.

"You should try it some time," she tells me. "With tits like yours, you could ask for more. At least thirty. Lift up your bra, two seconds, and the money's yours."

"I d-don't know if I c-could," I reply, realising that I've fallen back into my awkward old self for a minute. The words stumble out; I think it must be the shock of all these new developments. I don't know anything about parties, friends, boys, but I don't want to seem like a baby or a spoilsport. I want to fit in and be normal. I don't know if I can, though.

Megan shrugs loftily. "You don't need a degree, you know," she says, the sarcasm cutting like a knife. "And don't think you can have Ruben support you for ever. Or us girls. Sooner or later you'll have to return the favours; that's the way it works with us."

Return the favours.

She's right. I've accepted everything they've given me, their efforts to turn me into someone else, someone who doesn't spend her evenings cooped up at home studying. Ruben took me to the theatre, to dinner, to the beauty salon. The girls bought me clothes and helped me to look like less of a misfit. They accepted me even with my terrible shirts and baggy jeans, they took me into their midst and gave me somewhere to go when I didn't want to be at my mum's. They gave me a reason not to give up.

I couldn't live without them, not now. And once the Ship of Fools sinks, I'll need them more than ever. So it's only right that I do something in return.

I mull it over all night, while we're dancing, drinking and meeting new boys. Ruben's busy all the time, tied up with friends or guests as they arrive. I watch him and feel something growing inside me, the desire to make him happy, do something for him, return all the affection and attention he's given me for no reason. He looked into my eyes and saw beyond the bungling, pathetic little girl.

He smiles across the room at me and I feel all warm inside.

Dani comes over with a bunch of girls I don't know. They talk to Megan about setting up a group dance, they all agree on splitting the boys up between them.

"No chance," Megan interrupts, shutting them up. "It's a free contest, the one who pulls the most wins, just like we always do. No splitting. It's every girl for herself."

The others nod, although I notice a few aren't happy about it.

"What about her? Is she in or out?" one of the girls asks, lifting her chin to indicate me. She's giving me a worried look and I'm not sure why.

"If she wants," Megan says, smiling at me encouragingly. "Not that it's any of your business anyway."

They spread out quickly to find a spot in the middle of the room, climbing onto chairs, the coffee table and the sofa. The music changes and a track with a much louder beat comes on. The guys start to gather round as if they know what's about to happen.

"What's going on?" I ask Megan. It looks like the prep for a dance routine and you can feel the excitement in the air, almost like a first night at the theatre.

"Just you watch," she says. "If you like it, you can join us. If you do, you'll steal the show, no problem. Remember what I told you before."

Amid the guys cheering and the windows rattling to the music, Megan gets up on a chair and starts dancing. I've seen this happen at other parties, but it seems more electric this time. I move to the beat where I'm standing, not sure if I should join in or not. The new version of me would.

Ruben comes over to me, radiant, and eggs me on. "Go on, why don't you show them who's the prettiest?"

He looks so proud, as if he wants to show me off to the world and tell everyone, "She's mine." I smile but I still feel shy. He senses this and puts an arm round me, pulling something out of his pocket. A little blue pill with a dolphin on it sits in the palm of his hand.

"Try this," he suggests. "It'll help you to relax and have some fun."

I look at him, unsure. It looks harmless and the curve of the dolphin is reassuring.

Ruben puts it up to my lips, so I open my mouth and swallow it with a sip of my drink. Nothing happens.

I don't feel anything right away, not when Ruben takes me over to Megan, not when I get up on a chair beside her, and not even when I start dancing.

I dance and pick up the rhythm just like when I improvise with Electra. Little by little, everything in the room, all the faces, suddenly look brighter, more colourful, as if they're lit up from the inside. I feel like laughing and lift my arms, looking at Megan and trying to copy her, doing what she does, and it's only then that I realise she's got no clothes on, just her underwear. I look quickly across at Ruben, even though I'm having trouble controlling my brain and feel a sudden burst of energy that makes me cry out in joy. I hear myself scream, I see Ruben nodding approvingly amid bands of colour and stars shooting through my head, my dress slides down, and someone helps me step out of it.

I'm free. I dance and the music seeps through the pores of my skin. The boys love me and they edge closer, touching my shoes and the edge of my thong. Ruben smiles and can't take his eyes off me. I want to fly into his arms, I could fly, I'm sure of it, then Megan and the others take their bras off too and the crowd claps and cheers.

I can feel eyes, voices and banknotes sliding off me, and when I remove the final barrier between my skin and the world, the boys go wild and crowd round me. Someone touches me and I let them. It's a game and I'm learning the rules. I'm having fun and Ruben comes over to tell the guys to stand back but they insist and stick something in my thong, so Ruben tells me to get down, saying, "Come with me."

This is it. Now that he's seen what I'm willing to do for

him. Now that he knows how I can have fun as well, he'll kiss me. He leads me into a room and his voice floats in and out of my head, everything blazing and iridescent, as if I'm inside a rainbow. I'm lying on the bed, laughing.

Ruben touches me, but it's weird because I can feel his hands but he's not beside me, he's over by the door. I see different faces. I can feel my skin against someone else's. They touch me. They adore me. Someone mumbles in my muffled ears, "Never seen anything like it." Or something like that.

Then it all goes dark.

It's dark outside, but it's dark inside my head too.

I hear a distant voice calling me, but I know that even if I were to answer they wouldn't hear me. It's like I'm lost inside my head and I don't know how to get back. Yet I can still move, I feel my legs moving, fabric touching me, Ruben's warmth, his voice saying over and over, "It's okay."

I wake with a jump.

I'm sweating and my stomach's heaving. I throw up on the floor and pictures start filtering into my head like reeds pushing through a swamp. I must've been dreaming. I can't work out where I am until the furniture in my room, in my mum's house, comes into focus. It's bitterly cold. The window's wide open and the first light of day is filtering in. It was all a dream. Then I feel something beside me, on the bed. Pieces of paper. I take a better look, forcing my eyes to stay open.

It's money. A lot of money.

# 14

I'm blowing up balloons in the living room.

For every ten I tie up and let go, Matt pops at least one. It's no good telling him we need them for his mum and dad's party. He's running round the room like a madman throwing balloons up into the air, catching them then inevitably hitting them against any pointed object he can find.

"Matt, that's enough," his dad chides him. "Come and sit beside Aleksandra and behave yourself."

"*No!*"

"You know you're going to get into trouble if you carry on like that."

"No! No! No!"

I smile. I like how he fires out his *No!*s, dead set on what he wants and what he doesn't want. I didn't say "No" when I should have, and I feel so uncomfortable now it's making me jittery.

I wish I'd just shouted out *No!* when I had the chance.

I wish I'd said what I really thought.

But my mum wanted me to be part of her anniversary,

and I have the feeling she only wanted me here so I wouldn't feel excluded from a celebration that's nothing to do with me. This realisation only makes me feel worse, and the feeling of being on the outside, of being detached from everyone else, is so overwhelming I stammer like an idiot. I could try breathing exercises to calm myself down. All I'd have to do is concentrate on ignoring that massive number "5" printed on the balloons.

Five years of marriage to this nobody, who has no control over his son and lets him get away with anything. She didn't last twelve months with my dad, and they weren't even married when they had me.

I shouldn't dwell on these things, but they're the reason I should've said no and accepted the invitation to dinner at Thomas and Electra's instead.

When the guests start arriving, it gets worse. It hurts me to see my mum hug them all so affectionately. Her friends seem to care a lot about her and they greet me with the same enthusiasm, not seeming to notice my feeble handshake and look of embarrassment. It's like they're all pretending my being here is normal, but I know I'm the elephant in the room, and no matter how hard they try to make me feel I'm not, I know the truth.

I try to hide in a corner, but my mum's husband gives me the job of pouring out cocktails and serving them to the guests. I quaff a couple down quickly to calm my nerves and every time the bell rings I peer round in the hope that it's Carla and Megan.

The married couples all have children who are not

even out of primary school and there's no one here my age. It's so blatantly obvious that I was an accident, that my mum had me when she was too young to want me.

I feel tears pressing against my eyelids and a stab of pain forcing its way up from my chest.

Then the door opens and Carla comes in, looking splendid in a smart black dress, but without her daughter. I see her speaking fretfully to my mum who nods and puts an understanding hand on her shoulder. Then she walks her over to the buffet and helps her pick something to eat.

I wait for a few more minutes in the hope that Megan is just taking her time to get ready, but the door doesn't open and I feel increasingly alone.

I go over to her mum, a bit warily.

"Hi," I say. "Is everything going okay?"

She looks me up and down and her mouth twists into a grimace.

"How do you think it's going? Megan's out of control but you should know that, since you two are always together."

It's like she's accusing me but I refuse to feel guilty and I don't think she should criticise Megan. She's a good friend and that's enough for me.

"She's just lively," I say. "And she makes the most wonderful clothes ..."

Carla silences me with a wave of her hand. "Don't talk to me about clothes, please. I've stopped giving her money for material yet she still manages to get it. I really don't know how she does it," she says. She gulps down the contents of her wine glass in a couple of vigorous swigs and tops it up to the brim with some more. "Maybe you can tell me. But I think I know already. It's that ape of a boyfriend, that biker with no future."

I'm not that keen on Lee either, yet hearing Megan's mum belittle him makes me want to defend him. After all, she doesn't know him and she should show more respect for her daughter's feelings.

"Have you seen the bruises?" Carla implores. "And the scratches? Megan promises me that they've got nothing to do with him ..."

Luckily my mum joins us and then takes her friend away to show her something. I realise that Megan and her mum must have argued again and that's why Megan has refused to come to the party. So I go off to my room and check the window. Her light's on; she's definitely at home.

I call her mobile and she appears at the window, giving me a wave.

"How's the zombie bash going?" is the first thing she says.

"I c-can't t-take it any more," I reply. "Why d-don't you come over?"

"I argued with the bitch, so officially I'm not going to the party with her," she informs me. "You could come here."

"If I d-disappear my m-mum will n-notice." I think about it for a second then come up with a solution. "C-climb in the w-window. W-we can stay in my r-room."

"Okay."

I see her open the window wide, climb onto the sill and come through the hedge to get over to mine. She's wearing jeans and slippers, shivering as she jumps onto the frozen grass by my room.

"Oooh ... what's this, you trying to live like a cloistered nun?" she exclaims as soon as she comes in. "Seriously, Alek, you should try a bit harder with the decor. This place is grim."

She's right. I chose a wardrobe and shelves but didn't want any pictures for the walls or any decoration at all.

The truth is I wouldn't have known where to start and my mum just said, "Choose what you want." As if I would know what that was, after a life spent on a sofa bed. I like my daisy lamp on the desk, but the rest is just furniture, there to do its job.

"You could come with me some time to choose some more stuff," I suggest.

"Hey, great idea!" Megan cries, throwing herself down on my bed, crossing her legs. "Now that you're rich it'll be easy – you can buy whatever you like. How much did you make the other night?"

"I don't know," I reply.

I'd gathered the money together and stuffed it into the broken suitcase under my bed, the same place where I'd hidden the clothes from Ruben. I didn't even look at it, I was too scared. I'm not sure I know how it ended up in my room. I don't even remember how I got home.

"Come on, let's count it!" she says, clapping her hands

with excitement. "Your first night was amazing. You should be celebrating, what's with the long face?"

"I d-don't r-remember anything," I confess.

"Oh, that happens," she reassures me. Then she explains, "We did a bit of a strip and some guys wanted to touch you, but you'd dropped an E and must have blacked out. It happens. Sometimes it's better that way; when you come down you've got the money but zero memories."

"Wh-what about Ruben?" I ask, alarmed. If I let other boys touch me he'll be mad. Maybe that's why he hasn't replied to my texts this week.

Megan shrugs. "He's happy you were such a hit," she replies. "His friends complimented him on your body. Well, your tits, that is. I told you, they go mad for a great pair of tits."

"Oh."

It's all I manage to say as memories of Ruben at the door during the party start to come back to me.

It was Ruben who brought me home. Maybe getting completely out of it on a pill isn't that normal after all.

"Are you going to count your loot or not?" Megan insists. "You have to know how much you made; you won't know how much you can spend otherwise."

True.

I pull out the case and open it. I'm trembling a bit and Megan notices. She puts a hand on my shoulder, just like my mum did with her mum earlier. "Hey, are you okay? What's up?"

I'd like to say I'm disappointed that Ruben was happy to watch other guys touch me, but then I think that it must be the same for Lee, if he's Megan's boyfriend and they go to these parties together. Unless that's what he meant when he said "I want more" at Ruben's the other night. Maybe Lee was jealous and tried to tell Megan that, although I noticed that he didn't look upset when she was stripping.

I'm confused but I don't want to offend Megan. She looks genuinely happy for me and if she doesn't think all this is odd then it must just be me. I obviously don't understand how the group works yet. I just need to be patient and learn how to behave in all these different situations.

"N-nothing," I reply. "Nothing's up. H-here's the m-money."

I open the case and look at the crumpled notes. Megan grabs them and starts sorting them out, laying them out one at a time on her leg and flattening them with her hands.

"Ten, twenty, thirty, forty ..." she counts, straightening them and piling them up on the bed to her right. "One hundred and eighty!" she cheers at the end. "That's totally amazing, Alek! I told you you'd be the best. Just think, Dani's fuming – she only made sixty."

She hugs me tight and I hang onto her.

Someone knocks on the door and it opens right away. We jump apart. When I see my mum in the doorway, with Matt, I pray she doesn't see the money on the bed.

I feel like dying and my ears go red as she says, "I knew I'd find you here. Megan. Your mum was looking for you at home – she's going out of her mind with worry. Why don't you let her know you're here?"

"I'll call her right away," Megan says, smiling like an angel. I look at her and realise she's hidden the money so my mum won't see it.

I heave a sigh of relief and feel so grateful I've got her by my side.

My mum disappears again and Megan gives me a high five. We cackle like a couple of old crones. Then she asks me, "Do you mind if I take some money for the clothes I bought you at the shopping centre? I'm a bit short, got some material to buy, stuff like that."

"No problem," I say, and she pulls out some notes from the pile that has magically reappeared in her hand.

"I won't charge you for the belt," she says. "That's a present from me."

Later, when the house has gone quiet again, I put the money in the case and lie down on the bed to think, staring at the ceiling. No matter how much I think about how my life is changing, I can't get my head round it all. But maybe none of it matters as much as my friendship with Megan and my relationship with Ruben.

So, just before I fall asleep, I promise myself I'll do the right thing with the money, which is to buy Ruben a present and thank him for everything he does for me.

# 15

Helena won't look me in the eye.

She looks sad as she puts the final touches to the scenery that has come to life in her hands over the past few months. It's nearly ready to assemble on the stage now.

In contrast, she looks like she's falling apart. After her fit the other day, she hasn't shown any more signs of agitation, but I find this unnerving calm even worse. She seems to be wilting. When I walk past her, it's like I'm invisible. I'd like to say something to her but I don't know why she's so angry with me. I don't know what I've done to upset her like this.

While I'm backstage, I catch the dialogue between Gerald and Lord Illingworth. It's one of my favourite passages in the play and even though I'm not on stage, I know the lines by heart.

"Love is a very wonderful thing, isn't it?" says Gerald, young and in love with me, Hester.

"When one is in love one begins by deceiving oneself. And one ends by deceiving others," Lord Illingworth replies. "That is what the world calls a romance. But a really *grande passion* is comparatively rare nowadays."

"Can you help me with this cable, please?"

Jonah's voice distracts me from the play. He's messing about with his mixing desk again, that's all he ever does, even though there's not a lot needs arranging around here. I grab the cable he's holding out to me, wondering why he doesn't look for another job.

"Plug it in," he says, and I obey. "There's a similar one in my backpack, over there. Can you get it for me?"

He's being unusually polite, so I move cautiously, convinced he's got some silly prank lined up for me. I rummage around in his bag and have to pull everything out to find the cable amid the clutter. A CD slips out, entitled *Babbling Songs*. I also come across some pieces of plastic, like the one Jonah dropped on me during rehearsals, only these ones are intact and look like the things you use to play guitar with – plectrums.

I swipe it all, stuffing it into my pocket, and take the CD too, leaving only the case in his bag. A minor attempt at revenge, until something better comes along.

"No s-silly j-jokes today?" I ask as I hand him the cable he needs. He doesn't take his eyes off the levers and just shrugs, as if he too has an invisible weight on his shoulders. It scares me. "Y-you're losing y-your edge," I insist, waiting for a reaction.

"I've lost my inspiration, Lady Hester," he replies in a tired voice.

"You d-don't need inspiration t-to be a s-sound engineer," I retort sarcastically.

He doesn't flinch. His blond hair, come loose from his

146

bandana, flops over his face and casts a sinister shadow over his features. He throws me a fleeting glance, as if he doesn't really want to look at me, and his expression puzzles me; it's not part of his usual repertoire.

It's like Helena's. It seems sad.

Shaken, I go on stage, the sadness of the two of them sticking to me like the fabric of my imaginary dress, attaching itself to my performance.

"A woman who has sinned should be punished, shouldn't she?" I say, dolefully.

"More emphasis," Thomas calls from the stalls.

"A woman who has sinned should be punished, shouldn't she?" I exclaim, standing tall, rolling my shoulders back.

"Good."

But it's not good. It's impossible to be Hester properly. My mind's elsewhere. I'm not in part. But I persevere through to the end, in a sort of trance, and I'm relieved when rehearsals are over.

I head to the bathroom and glimpse Jonah in the back corner with Helena. It looks like he's whispering to her and she's listening while she works. I haven't got time to think about what they're up to, though. Ruben's waiting for me outside.

But the picture stays in my mind as I change, pull on a short skirt, a loose, low-cut top and heels, and then do my make-up squinting in the dim, dusty light of the bulb above the grimy mirror.

I think about it in the car too, as Ruben races along

roads that I don't know, talking all the time on his phone. We drive over to Lee's house and Megan's there too. She's got an elated, drunken look on her face, like she's ready for a wild night. She hugs me as she climbs in the back and that makes me feel better, dispersing the gloom and psyching me for the party, along with a gulp of vodka. Ruben's car has a tiny fridge built into the back of the driver's seat, so Megan and I can serve ourselves, toast each other and cast aside all thoughts of the world outside.

Ruben is very affectionate tonight. We go into his friend's house and he holds me tight, his arm round my shoulders pulling me close. His heat and his smell wash over me. He kisses my neck a few times before going off to greet the host of the party, then comes back with two tall glasses of champagne. We toast together, just the two of us.

"You had me worried the other night," he says, with an intent look. "The pill I gave you shouldn't have had that effect. I'm sorry. I bet you felt really bad."

I shake my head firmly. "No, not at all. I got over it really quickly," I reassure him. "I w-was just w-worried you were annoyed."

He smiles. "Why on earth would I be annoyed? It was all going great until you blacked out," he says, taking my hand. "You were amazing. My friends can't stop talking about you."

I look at him, doubtful, and he hugs me.

"We're here to have fun, remember?" he says gently. "Don't worry about anything. I'm right by your side."

I let him squeeze me. All the knots I've been carrying around since the night of the strip, of the blackout, seem to melt away in a tidal wave of affection. I drink a few more glasses of champagne with Ruben and let the bubbles go to my head. I dance with him, I dance with Megan, then when I notice a lot of couples are moving into quiet corners to kiss and touch each other, I give Ruben a telling look.

I want to be with him.

He understands. He takes my hand and we disappear into an empty room. He shuts the door and sits on the bed, signalling me to sit beside him.

"Do you want to try something new?"

Tonight I want to be perfect. I've had just enough alcohol to feel tipsy but not sick; my brain has loosened up but is still engaged. I nod, but I don't dare say I'd like him to kiss me.

He's already unbuttoning his shirt and I take in his perfect, muscular chest, the perfect place for me to hide.

He takes off his jeans and boxers and lies on the bed, naked. He smiles at me. "Are you embarrassed?" he asks.

I'm dying of embarrassment.

"No," I say.

Then I get undressed, because I think that's what I'm supposed to do. I stand there in my underwear and look at him.

"Kiss me," he says, and I'm about to bring my face to his, my heart racing, when I notice that he's looking down. He's not looking at my lips. His gaze has stopped between his legs. The scene in the bathroom at Ruben's house, a few weeks ago, flashes into my head, blinding me. I remember Dani with her head between that guy's legs.

But I don't know how to do it, so I hesitate.

"It's easy," Ruben says, ignoring my unease and being kind instead of telling me I'm pathetic. "Come on, I'll help you."

He does everything lovingly. I imagine I'm kissing his lips, it makes it easier, and hearing him sigh with pleasure spurs me on even though my jaw's hurting and, at times, I feel like I can't breathe. He places a hand on my shoulder, stroking my hair, pushing my head down gently.

"Take everything off," he murmurs, and I obey. He touches me, still groaning, and I want to make love to him, whatever happens, but I keep kissing him between his legs until he asks me, in a strangled voice, "All the way? Can I?"

I feel myself go red. I don't really know what he means. So I just smile and he takes it as a yes. We go all the way.

I'm not sure if I like it to be honest, I don't know if it's better than the kiss I was expecting, but I do know that, right now, Ruben's mine and he needs me. While I've got my head between his legs, he keeps groaning and saying how special I am, then he spasms and liquid fills my mouth.

Afterwards he stays lying on the bed, looking at me

like I'm truly special, so I lie down beside him and think that, at the end of the day, as long as I can be beside him and feel that I've done the right thing for him, that's fine by me.

# 16

"You've changed, Alek."

Camilla says it in the same matter-of-fact way that she calls my mum "the flake", like it's a simple statement and not an opinion open to debate.

"Something's happening to you," she adds, staring at me and silently imploring me to confide in her. It's always been really easy with her, my old school mate. I would tell her about my broken family when there was no one else I could talk to or when I was afraid of being called different because I lived with my gran. Camilla is a good listener. But she's also someone who makes black and white judgements. Right now, I don't have anything black and white for her.

"I'm going out with a boy," I say, using the only piece of information that's not swimming around in the sea of confusing, conflicting thoughts that's in my head. "I've been going to a few parties, you know, to have some fun."

"That's all very well, but you failed another test today," she says, sternly. "It's not like you. You've always been so careful about your marks. And look at how tired you are, you're miles away."

"You're r-right," I admit. "I've been g-going to bed l-late. But I'm g-going to c-catch up before the end of t-term."

"You'd better, otherwise you'll have to look for someone else to sit next to. I'm not failing just to keep you company," she says.

For all her front, I can sense the concern in her voice. I can see it on her face.

It's a relief when she disappears off to her music lesson, leaving me on my own for lunch. My head feels heavy because of all the alcohol I drank last night at Megan's house as we sat in her room, pretending to do our homework to keep Carla happy. Not to mention the pill I took later when I sneaked out to see Ruben. It wasn't as powerful as usual, but there are parts of the night I can't remember, leaving me with only scary fragments of memories that I can't make any sense of. Like a jigsaw puzzle with too many bits missing or broken, preventing you from seeing the whole picture.

But I do know that the suitcase is filling up with money.

I know that Ruben's friends regularly seek me out, that I'm some kind of star in the group, and that when we strip at someone's house, I always make more money than the other girls. Every now and then they ask to touch me. Occasionally someone wants to be touched. Megan showed me how to do it on my first guy, who paid double because there were two of us playing with him. She said, "We're all friends. You give them something, they give you something." She winked at me and added, lowering her voice, "The great thing is it only lasts a few seconds. After which you've got fifty quid in your pocket."

When I do it with my mouth, I do it alone the way that Ruben taught me.

I like touching Ruben, but now that only happens at the end of the night, after everyone's gone. That's what I wait for with an anxiety that devours me, and that's why I dance and drink in the meantime, trying to have fun and keep up with Megan, who always seems to be buzzing.

I miss Ruben so much, every minute of the day. A smile from him fills my heart with joy, but then I wait for hours on end for him to call me, to come looking for me, to be together for a bit, alone, not in the middle of the chaos at the parties.

Dealing with all these thoughts at school is torture.

When my head's clear, in the calm light of day, I feel naked. As if everyone's looking at me and can see my secrets. A boy stopped me in the corridor at school the other day and said, "I'll top up your mobile if you come to the toilets with me for five minutes."

I ran away, even though I couldn't go very fast in my tottery heels, and it felt like all the other students were lining the corridors, watching me and knowing why I was running.

Megan told me that my clothes are attracting attention but I've not to worry because it's up to me who I go with.

She said, "Just say no."

A week ago, someone wrote "Megan and her mates are slags" in huge letters across the mirrors in the girls' toilets. The caretaker had washed it off by the next day, and Megan didn't seem that upset. She just said that people are jealous because boys like us, and if she finds out who wrote it, she'll smash their face in.

Instead of going to the canteen, I go out into the courtyard and head over to the others, who are clustered together in a secluded corner. They're smoking, but I don't like cigarettes so I accept the bottle of rum they're passing around instead, as they pick at a bag of crisps or paint their nails.

I stand out here in the cold, listening to the girls' chatter and letting the drink slide through me like a painkiller.

At one point, Megan raises her hand to show us her ring, sparkling on her finger in the flat winter sun. "What do you think?"

"Is it real?" Kayley asks, moving closer.

"Of course it is," Megan replies, proudly. "It's an engagement ring. Lee has finally made up his mind. He's realised I'm the only woman for him."

"Wow, it's fabulous," Anna exclaims, her voice tinged with envy as she hugs Megan. "Congratulations."

"You're amazing, Megan," Kayley squeals.

"Thanks."

I wonder if Ruben will give me one too, when our relationship is more solid. I would give anything for him to give me a ring instead of all those clothes I have to hide and shoes I can't wear during the day.

"If your mum sees it, she'll kill you," Dani sneers. "Won't she be thrilled to welcome a mechanic into the family?"

Megan's face clouds over and she glares at Dani.

The others turn all jittery and try to change the subject. But Megan gets off the wall she's sitting on and faces Dani, a look of cold contempt in her eyes. "Want to know something? You're not worth a toss as a friend or as a whore," she hisses. "Don't think you'll get an invite to the next party."

Dani goes pale, all her swagger gone. Her lip trembles. "Come off it, Megan, I was only messing about," she mumbles, slurring her words. "You know I have to be there."

"You should've thought of that before. And you're getting too old, the guys aren't interested any more. You do too many drugs, you can see it on your face," Megan adds, harsh and fierce.

I've never seen her like this. It's just as well it all sounds so muffled to my ears because it's scary enough as it is. She's like someone else. I don't know what she means by "too old", either. Dani's barely a year and a half older than us, she should remind Megan of that. Instead she starts to cry and stumbles off. No one tries to stop her or catch up with her.

The silence that follows is like a black hole swallowing me up. After a bit, Megan starts talking about the engagement ring again, as if Dani were just a distant memory, and then my phone goes, dragging me out of the rum-soaked abyss I've fallen into.

It's Ruben.

I want to scream down the phone, come and get me, come and take me away from here. I can't stand that Dani's gone and I don't know why, but it feels like it's because of me and my friendship with Megan. Or maybe it's the alcohol playing havoc with my mood, as Ruben always says, and making me cry. All it would take is a pill to get going again, but I don't have one on me here.

"Hey, Alek," he says in his soft voice.

"Hiya," I murmur, on the verge of tears.

"Listen, do you fancy skipping school today?" he asks cheerfully. "Just this once. I'll come and pick you up and we'll go and see a friend of mine. Then we'll go out to dinner, by the beach. Do you fancy it?"

It's the only thing I want right now and I accept so eagerly that he starts to laugh. I quickly say goodbye to the others and rush over to the place in the fence that's hidden behind some evergreen shrubs. I climb over, shaking off the dizziness from the drink, and run to where I'm supposed to meet him, a couple of bends down the road from the school, shoving a chewing gum in my mouth as I go.

When I get in the car I throw my arms around Ruben's neck. He hugs me, then pushes me away, saying, "What's up?"

"D-Dani's gone," I cry. "Megan kicked her out."

He smiles and caresses my head. "Don't let it upset

you. Dani tried it on with Lee, that's why Megan's angry with her," he explains.

"R-really?" I ask, drying my eyes with the tissue he gives me.

He drives off, reassuring me that everything's okay. Dani's a rotten apple, he says, and you can't have rotten apples in a group. You need to be able to trust each other, to count on your friends, without having to watch your back all the time.

He's right. I didn't know Dani liked Lee. I would be mad too if she tried it on with Ruben. So Megan was right to do what she did; I shouldn't have doubted her.

I relax. There's some nice, upbeat music on the radio and we're driving through the suburbs on roads that lead to the beach. It's a long way but Ruben's car is fast and I really want to walk on the deserted beach with him, looking at the seagulls, at the expanse of ocean. He takes my hand as we drive and every cell in my body seems to loosen up. I trust him. I want to be near him. Every time I see him, I know I'd do anything not to lose him. Even the idea of him not being by my side is too much to bear.

"Listen, Alek," he tells me as we pull into a piece of open ground in front of some sort of industrial building. "A friend of mine wants to meet you. He's heard a lot about you but can't come to our parties because he works long hours. Do you mind?"

I take a deep breath to prepare myself. I know what he means. Now I can decipher sentences that were once completely incomprehensible to me.

"Do I have to?" I ask, falteringly. I feel sick and the light feels like it's blinding me. The others aren't here, there's no music like at the parties and this place is dismal.

"Of course not," he reassures me. "I'd promised him but I can tell him it's off," he says, calmly. He's staring straight ahead though, disappointment clouding his face.

My heart starts to break again. I'm scared if I don't meet his friend he'll take me home without going to the beach with me. That he'll say I'm too young for him again.

So I smile and start acting. "It's okay. Let's go."

I get out the car and I'm no longer Aleksandra. I'm that better girl. I can sway my hips. I can walk in heels without stumbling. My make-up's perfect – I'm even better at it now than Megan. She says it's my artistic side finding a new means of release. Ruben takes my hand and my confidence doubles because the touch of his fingers makes me feel like I'm his and he'll always be by my side to protect me.

We go round the back of the building to some sort of pre-fab. A man in a crumpled shirt and tie with a hard hat on comes out. There's no one else around. It's a building site but there are no other labourers.

"Hey, Ruben," the man exclaims, coming towards us. He has greying hair, a bit of a belly, and is wearing sunglasses.

"Good afternoon," Ruben greets him, shaking his hand. "This is Aleksandra, the girl I was telling you about."

"My pleasure," the man says, nodding at me. "Come with me."

I follow him into the cabin while Ruben waits outside. It's cold inside even though there's a heater on in the corner.

The man takes his hard hat and jacket off then sits down on a swivel chair. He's still wearing his sunglasses.

"Let me see," he says, opening my jacket. I'm wearing a light blouse underneath and he unbuttons it in a flash.

"Sweet Jesus," he murmurs, and he starts touching me. He unhooks my bra and unzips his trousers and it's time for me to step outside of myself. I leave my body and look down from above. The man's moaning like they all do. The better girl than me knows what she's doing; she's learned quickly and gets straight to work. I watch awkwardly from the ceiling, waiting for the girl and the man to finish, ears burning and heart hammering in my chest.

"Do you want something to drink?" the man says a few minutes later, after he's washed his hands.

I'm a bit dazed, having lost my bearings for a second. Then the room comes back into focus. I'm sitting on the floor, half-naked. I try to yank my clothes back on but my hands are trembling with the cold.

"Okay," I reply, accepting the beer he takes out of a fridge in the corner. I take the rolled-up wad of notes he gives me too. I stand up and go outside, sipping from the bottle even though I don't really want it, but at least it gives me something to hold onto. Ruben's right outside the door and he tells me to wait for him in the car.

Looking out from the car, I see him talking to the man then slapping him on the back like old mates. The sun through the window warms me up and the cool beer gets rid of the sour taste in my mouth. I'm still gripping the money and automatically open my hand to count it. Two hundred pounds. That's much more than I usually get.

As we drive away, Ruben whistles along to the radio and I wonder why a working man like that is willing to pay so much for a young girl like me.

"Alek, Alek," Ruben chirps happily. "You're amazing. You floored him, literally. He says he wants to see you again."

We get to the coast and the sun's setting. We get out at the seafront and I rub my eyes, thinking that I can't be seeing it properly, because even though the sky is awash with colour, the sea looks as black as ink, like a deep well, a place of no return.

# 17

I messed up again.

"It's an easy line, Aleksandra," says Thomas patiently. "You've said it a thousand times."

"I kn-know," I reply, lowering my head. I don't feel well, my stomach's lurching and my head is pounding. I ask Thomas if I can go home early. I think I must have a temperature or maybe I'm just tired.

I collect my things and hear Electra ask Jonah, "Can you read Aleksandra's lines, please?"

"It'll be an honour to replace Lady Hester," he replies.

The word "replace" rubs like sandpaper but I'm incapable of reacting today.

As I head behind the curtain, I bump into Jonah making his way on stage. He grabs my wrist and hisses under his breath, "What on earth's got into you?"

He's angry but I've no idea why. I wrench my hand free and reply, "G-give me some p-peace, would you."

He shouts after me, "This ain't peace, sister. Can't you see?"

I don't listen to him.

I can hardly stand up, so I take off my heels and go out of the theatre barefoot, paying no attention to the cold or to the fact that I'm in the middle of the road. I just want to go to bed and sleep.

I want to switch off my brain, because it's buzzing and racing at an unbearable speed. My vision is blurred and the images it presents to me are confusing. It'll be a relief to close my eyes.

When I get home, my mum jumps up from the table and comes towards me. "Where's Matt?" she asks.

I don't know what she's talking about. I look at her, blinking, and she reminds me, her voice rising. "You were supposed to pick him up, opposite the theatre."

Memories of his friend's birthday party come creeping back but fail to trigger a response.

"You offered, yesterday," she insists.

I'd like to say I'm sorry, that I'm really, really sorry.

But I don't say anything, and instead fight the nausea and sense of detachment I'm feeling. I'm here, but I'm not really here. I'm floating and sinking at the same time, sinking and floating with no hope of stopping.

My mum grabs the phone and calls her husband, telling him to pick up Matt. Then she calls the friend's house to let the mum know. I'm about to walk away, the sense of guilt weighs heavy but it's not enough to stop me.

"Wait," my mum says. "Where have you been?"

She's shouting and it throws me. The fog lifts a little as I reply, "At rehearsals, you know that."

"Are you telling me the truth?" she says, imploring. She's just inches away and I look into her eyes for the first time. They're so similar to mine it's like looking into a mirror.

"Yes."

"There was sick in the hedge in front of the house this morning," she says, matter-of-fact. "Did you sneak out last night, without saying anything?"

"N-no," I lie. "The s-sick's not m-mine."

She sighs and shakes her head. "The cleaning lady found a towel under your bed."

I pray with all my heart she didn't open the case and find the money too. And the clothes and shoes.

"It was covered in sick," she adds. "Was that not yours either?"

I don't know what to say. I'd rather not say anything. I want to sleep or pass out, anything to get me away from all this, to make it stop.

She tries a softer voice. "Alek, what's going on?" She wrings her hands, attempts a diagnosis. "Are you bulimic? Are you ill but don't want to tell us?"

The "us" throws me. There is no us, there's only me and them.

"I-I'm f-fine," I reply automatically. "I did have a sore s-stomach but it's all r-right n-now."

She doesn't believe me, I can tell. She keeps staring at me, as if she might find the truth written on my face. Right now, I don't think my face shows anything but emptiness.

"I don't want to be on your case, Alek," she goes on. "My mum was always on at me and it didn't get her anywhere. But if I'm to treat you like an adult, I need to be sure you are one."

I don't like her talking about Gran so I clamp my mouth shut.

"Even though you've never wanted to confide in me, you have to know that I'm here to listen and help you, whatever you're going through," she says, her voice a low mumble.

Sixteen years of loneliness spring to mind.

Violent, painful and rapid flashbacks that take my breath away, triggered by what my mum has just said.

Sixteen years without her. Years of waiting for my birthday, the only day we ever saw each other, so that I could be with her. Years in which I walked the streets of this town hoping I'd bump into her while hoping I wouldn't. Tears well up and anger explodes inside me. I hate scenes. I never say what I think. Yet the words erupt as if they'd turned rotten inside me and needed to be spat out.

"*I* never wanted to?" I yell. "You were the one who didn't want me in your life. And you expect me to trust you now? It's too late! Way too late!" I'm shouting at the top of my voice and I can feel my throat burning. "I can leave if you want, just say the word. I'll pack my case right away. After all, I know it's what you want, an excuse to get rid of me again." Lowering my voice, I add, "I'm used to it by now. I don't care any more."

I run into my bedroom before she has time to reply. From the look in her eyes, I've obviously hit a nerve, so maybe she'll finally stop lying and pretending now. I pull out my suitcase and stuff all the money into the side pocket. Then I start throwing in the clothes and shoes haphazardly, not really aware of what I'm doing.

The door opens.

"Aleksandra."

I turn round. My mum's in the doorway, a strange look on her face.

She hands me a book. "I wanted to give you this at a better time. I had hoped it would be a present for a special occasion or for when we're a bit closer," she says. "But maybe it's right that you read it now. It's the diary I kept for you when Gran wouldn't let me see you."

I don't move. I don't feel anything. I wish she'd just leave me in peace. But she takes a few steps towards me and places a blue book on the white bedspread. "Read it when you want," she says. "And when you feel ready, we can talk about it."

She disappears again and closes the door softly.

I brush my fingers over the diary, my mum's words echoing round my head. What did she say? What did she say about my gran?

I open the cover and read the first line handwritten in blue ink in big, round letters.

There's a date.

9th July.

My birthday.

There's a photo of me below it, aged one.

And below that a few scribbled lines, written in a hurry.

*Aleksandra is one today and I'm not with her. I shouldn't have let myself be talked into leaving her, anything would be better than this, whatever the price. I told Hadrijan that I want to go and get my baby but he told me to wait, that as soon as he finds a good job we'll go together.*

I can't go on. But I have to. This is the truth I've been longing to know and all of a sudden I'm not sure I can handle it. Not now. Maybe it really is too late. Maybe there are scars that just can't be healed. I look at the baby girl smiling out from the faded photo. Does she know what's going on around her? Does she know her mum and dad have gone? Is she already wondering if her gran will get tired of her and leave her too?

She looks happy, a normal baby girl. A baby with only half a history, until now.

I read on, pressing a hand on my stomach to dull the pain, forcing myself to breathe.

I discover that my gran sent my mum reams of photos over the years, all of which have been carefully preserved in this diary.

I also discover that my mum left my dad in the end because he wouldn't make up his mind to come and get me. She came back to my gran's with social services, but they wouldn't grant her custody of me because she had no job and no qualifications. I stayed with my gran for the next six years and my mum only saw me a few times.

She went back to school for me. She found a job and a house and kept studying because there was only one thing she wanted. Me.

*I want my daughter to be proud of me. I want to be able to give her the life she deserves.*

The problem is, I don't believe any of it. I'd like to, but I can't. I've been here all the time, in the same city as her – she could've come to get me a lot earlier. But she just kept ignoring me and keeping me at a distance. As I read her words, I realise it's a distance that might be too big to overcome now.

But I read on like a zombie, feeling only exhaustion and indifference. She wrote me some poems, beside the photos she kept of me. Then, on my sixth birthday, she made this note.

*I went to my mum's today, convinced I was going to take Aleksandra back. All the paperwork was ready. I'd been waiting for this moment for years. It was her birthday party and children were running all over the flat. Aleksandra took a tumble at one point and grazed her knee. I went over to help her but she pushed me aside and limped over to her gran to be consoled. She kept saying, Gran, Gran, Gran. It was like I was invisible. My mum insisted I leave Aleksandra with her, that by now she had her home and shunting her somewhere new would only upset her more. She's right. I went home in tears but I realise now it's the right thing to do. Aleksandra is fine. I'm no one to her. I'm not the one she'd run to if she were to hurt herself again.*

I should feel pain, joy, or maybe even sympathy. But I

don't. I only feel wounded, detached. Why didn't anyone ever ask me what I wanted? Why didn't my gran tell my mum how I used to ask about my mum and dad every night, wanting to know when they'd be coming for me? Why didn't she tell me my mum had tried to take me back?

Who should I believe? The woman who raised me or the woman who left me?

I hate this. I hate all of them. But, more than anything, I hate myself, because if I hadn't shoved her aside that day, if I'd let her take care of my grazed knee, maybe things would've been different. I don't even remember that I did that, I was just a little girl used to relying on someone who wasn't my mum.

I have a huge knot inside but tears won't come to undo it. I hurl the diary down, in fury, and a few loose photos fall out. One lands right at my feet. It's a picture of a boy smiling. There's a name written above it in felt pen – *Hadrijan*, it says. He looks like me. I always thought he'd be different and, seeing him now, so alien yet so familiar, is devastating. He has the same bushy auburn hair as me and the same smile, shaky, almost sad.

I pick up his photo and run my finger over it, tears falling now.

I can say the word over and over in my head – *Daddy Daddy Daddy* – and finally put a face to that word.

But it doesn't make me feel any better.

# 18

I drag my suitcase along with all my might and think that maybe one jammed wheel isn't as bad as two. I also think that I could stop and buy a new case, but I don't want to waste any time. The train leaves in twenty minutes and I don't want to risk missing it.

I'm leaving.

When my mum gets home tonight, I won't be there. I don't know why that diary has upset me so much, but her giving it to me like that felt like a way to make me feel guilty or to accuse my gran.

I thought about it all night. She could've insisted but she didn't. She could've asked to see me more often, but she settled for birthdays. So, whatever happened between her and my gran, it doesn't change what happened to me.

In the half-hour it takes the train to get into town, I try to block it from my mind and focus my thoughts on Ruben instead. I tried to call him, but he rang off really quickly saying he was busy studying. I can't wait, though; he's the only one who can help me or tell me what to do. I have to see him, talk to him, tell him what I've decided.

After a short bus ride, I get to the flat where he lives during the week and buzz the intercom. The traffic in this unfamiliar city is rumbling noisily around me, but the seconds separating me from Ruben's voice are ticking away to the insistent, consuming rhythm of my beating heart.

"Who is it?"

"R-Ruben, it's me," I reply.

There's silence for a few seconds then he mumbles, "Me who?"

"A-A-A ..."

I can't speak. My tongue's in knots. Too many emotions are swirling around inside me. I kick the wall in frustration.

"Aleksandra?" he fills in for me, sounding surprised.

"Y-yes," I exclaim, relieved.

Another silence follows and I start to panic.

"Wait there, I'm coming right down," he says eventually.

I wait and wait and wait, biting my nails and ruining the polish. The front door finally opens and I'm so happy to see Ruben I sweep him up in a massive hug, clinging onto him.

"Hey, hang on," he says, confused. "What's going on? What are you doing here? You should be at school."

I start to cry. He spots my suitcase and takes me by the shoulders. "Aleksandra. Will you tell me what's going on?"

He sounds alarmed, which is not what I was expecting.

He pulls me inside the main door and shuts it. "You shouldn't have come here. You should've called."

"I did, don't you remember?" I say, sounding petulant. "B-but you w-were busy."

He sighs. "Try to calm down and tell me what's wrong."

I tell him about my mum, the diary, my sixth birthday and the photo of my dad. I don't know what's spilling out, a torrent of disconnected syllables, but he seems to understand because he nods while gesturing with his hand for me to lower my voice.

"Yeah, that must've been hard to swallow," he says, his voice distracted and quiet. "But you still shouldn't come here during the day."

I look into his sky blue eyes and manage to say, without stuttering, "I want to stay with you."

I smile uncertainly then feel like dying when he shakes his head and exclaims, "Are you out of your mind? You're just a kid, I'll get into loads of trouble. Your mum will be looking for you." He grabs the suitcase. "I'll take you home, come on."

I grab his arm to stop him and shout, "No!" Then, lowering my voice, I add, "P-please, just a f-few nights. I d-don't want to g-go back to my mum's. I'm b-begging you."

He tilts my chin up towards him with his hand. "Alek, you want to keep seeing me, don't you?"

The question scares me. I nod. "Y-yes."

"Well," he says. "If you stay here and your mum calls

the police and they find out I'm hiding you, we won't be able to see each other any more. Do you understand?"

I hadn't thought of that. My plan had seemed perfect; my mind had raced beyond the next few days to a lifetime together. I watch him put my case into the boot of his car, ready to take me home, and it looks more like he's sorting out a problem than wanting to help me.

I'd like to argue, but his reasoning has backed me into a corner.

"Go on, get in the car," he urges, but I can't move. I really don't have anywhere else to go now, there's nowhere I feel safe.

Before we get in, Ruben buzzes his flat. I hear a woman's voice answer.

"Tess, sorry, something's come up," he says. "I have to rush over to the court for Dad. I'll be back in an hour."

"Oh. Okay," the voice replies, muffled and annoyed. "But hurry up. I have to be at the dentist's at three –"

"Yes, yes, of course," he says. "Don't worry. I'll be quick."

The intercom clicks shut. Ruben turns towards the car and I follow him, dragging my feet. "Who w-was that g-girl in your f-flat?" I ask in a strangled voice.

The avalanche of agony is lifted off me when he answers, "My sister. She's a proper pain in the neck. If she saw me with you she'd tell my parents."

The avalanche returns. "Wh-what's wr-wrong with me? Why w-would it matter if sh-she t-told y-your parents?" I say, thinking how Ruben met my mum on our very first date.

"Aleksandra, please," he says, exasperated. "Don't make things difficult. Please? I'm bending over backwards for you, the least you could do is not add to the stress."

I shut up. I don't want him to get angry. I take his hand but he pulls away.

"Don't go doing things on your own," he continues, firmly. "When you have a problem, calm down and either call me or Megan. You're a good girl, and good girls need to think straight."

"Okay," I mumble, disheartened. I want to cry, but then he strokes the back of my neck.

"Don't worry," he soothes. "It'll pass. You'll see."

He caresses my hair and the tears disappear, my heart's no longer racing.

"I'm s-sorry," I tell him, suddenly worried. "I d-didn't want to get in the way of your st-studying."

"It doesn't matter," he reassures me. "As long as I know you're going home much calmer. Are you?"

"Yes," I lie. "I'm b-better n-now."

"Excellent," he says. "Open the glove compartment then."

I obey. Inside there are some papers, with a yellow parcel on top. "It's for you," Ruben tells me. "I wanted to give it to you tomorrow, at Lee's party, but maybe it will make you feel better now."

I unwrap it, a smile on my lips, feeling silly but lucky at the same time. I find a black babydoll, lacy and see-through.

"Thanks," I mumble. "It's b-beautiful."

"It'll look incredible on you," he states. "Bring it tomorrow, will you? We're staying over at Lee's."

My eyes go wide. "R-really? You mean all f-four of us?"

"Yes."

"C-can I s-sleep with y-you?"

"Of course."

I forget all the rest. We drive the whole way home in silence, with only the songs playing on the radio to accompany our thoughts. I'm certain we're thinking the same thing. We'll be together tomorrow night; we'll wake up together, maybe after making love. I tremble at the thought and imagine what it'll be like to be in his arms with all the time in the world ahead of us.

My mum's car is in the driveway.

"Sh-shit," I exclaim before I can stop myself. "She c-came home early."

"Don't worry. I'll deal with it," Ruben says, calm and decisive. He parks, gets out the car and lifts my case out of the boot. Then he takes my hand and walks me up to the door. He's the one who rings the bell and smiles at my mum when she opens it, clearly wondering what he's doing there at this time of day.

He's the one who explains everything, acting as if it were all true. "She thought you were at work, so she rang me. She didn't feel well during P.E."

"And why the suitcase?" my mum asks, sceptical. But I sense that she likes Ruben and is willing to trust him.

"Oh, she has some stuff for the theatre in it," he answers. "For rehearsals."

"Costumes," I add. "I'll t-take them t-tomorrow."

She swallows it and lets me in, then lingers outside with Ruben. I hear her whispering but can't make out what they're saying. Then she laughs, relieved, and I know she won't ask any questions and I can go to my room. But not before saying goodbye to my boyfriend. The sun is streaking his chestnut hair with gold and lighting up his confident smile.

Not whispering any more, he says to my mum, "We'd like to stay over at Lee's, so we don't have to drive home late at night, you know, after the party. It would be safer."

She nods, tells him that I can go and wishes him the best of luck for his studies and forthcoming exams. Ruben gets in the car, indicates and pulls carefully away from the kerb, much slower than usual.

I don't know if I'll be able to wait until tomorrow to see him. I'm so excited, my first night with him without having to climb out the window and back in at daybreak, scared I'll get caught. When I get into my bedroom, I pull the babydoll out of my jacket pocket and try it on in front of the mirror, this see-through lacy thing that caresses my skin and shows my body beneath it, and makes me feel sexy. I'll knock Ruben out tomorrow. He'll forget today's childish scene in an instant and won't be able to drag himself away from me. I'll be irresistible, his woman again.

I'm about to get dressed when I notice a piece of folded-up paper on the floor. It must've fallen out of my jacket. I pick it up and I'm about to throw it away, thinking it's a receipt, when I realise there's handwriting shining through it. I open it and my blood runs cold, an unbearable chill coursing through my veins. I rip the paper into shreds and throw them in the bin, pushing them down to the bottom. I don't know who wrote the message or how they managed to get it into my pocket. I don't recognise the writing. All I know is that the words echo round my head for the rest of the day, and keep me awake at night.

*I know what you're doing, I can see it on your face. You'll come to a nasty end if you don't stop now or speak to someone about it.*

*A friend.*

I pull my pillow over my head, hoping it'll drown out the clamour of those words. It doesn't work.

# 19

Lee's place is a nice flat in the centre of town. You can see the city all lit up from the top floor and the rows of identical tower blocks look prettier at night, as if made of lights instead of concrete.

We're getting ready for the strip. Megan passes us all a pill and a glass of neat gin and lemon, then raises hers for a toast.

"To gorgeous girls. To us!" she cries in ecstacy.

There's a new girl beside her. I've never seen her in the group before, but she looks much younger than the rest of us. Megan introduced her as her cousin. Her flat, childlike body is dressed up in skimpy, sexy clothes, making me feel uncomfortable, at least until I down the pill and the gin and can finally relax.

As I lift my drink, I see Megan put her arm round her, and her cousin smiles back nervously. Megan's words are muddled as they float over to me, and I let them slide off because I don't want them to leave their mark on me.

"If anyone asks how old you are, just say sixteen. If they find out your real age, it might put them off. Boys like to pretend, and we're here to give them what they want."

The young girl nods. Megan's busy trying to straighten her padded bra and I can see that she has almost no chest.

"Do whatever you feel like," she continues. "Dance, have fun, make them want you. They love baby-faces like yours, you know that?"

The girl grins, apparently proud of this. "And when should I take my clothes off?" she asks, impatient and a bit jittery. I look away, shocked by the ease with which she says it and the fact that Megan is being so direct.

"Watch us and learn," Megan replies, winking. "If you do what you're told, tomorrow we'll go shopping together."

With that, we get up on the chairs and tables and start dancing.

The room's so crowded the windows have been opened to let some air in, even though it's freezing outside. My movements are smooth, my mind empty. I dance for the boys reaching out to me and sticking money into my shoes and my thong, but my eyes are fixed on Ruben. I'm here for him. Thinking of him holds me together and stops me from collapsing into a million pieces on the floor. The music carries me, it's easy to let go, to close my eyes and hide behind this better person than myself, this girl who moves and lets people touch her, always smiling.

Megan's cousin is dancing near me, but I try not to look at her. Ruben smiles across from the other side of the room, nodding his approval. I dance even harder, goading the throng of boys around me. Everything is bright, radiant, blurry. I'm a star and shouts reach my ears from boys who want me, cheering me, telling me I'm hot, hot, hot.

One licks my belly button, grabbing my bum. I grasp his hair and pull aside the elastic of my thong, like I've seen Megan do, and wait for him to slip in a banknote.

What a dickhead, I think. But I smile. He's worthless and I'm calling the shots here. He's paying to see me dance because I'm irresistible, I'm sexy, and I can hold these guys in the palm of my hand just by showing them my tits. I touch them and the guys go wild, tucking more money in, throwing it at me. It's so easy. *So* easy.

When we finish, I climb down from the chair and gather up the money. I go into the box room where our stuff is to put it in my bag. I don't even bother to put my clothes back on. Even if I wanted to I couldn't. My legs and arms are so light right now I can't feel them, it's amazing that I can even stay upright. I'm giggling for no reason.

Ruben comes up behind me and takes my arm. His clothes rub against my skin and his heat invades me. He pushes me into the room and shuts the door. I keep giggling and wrap my arms around him as he kisses me, licking my neck, my chest, my shoulders.

I'm ready.

I want to make love to him. He pulls my thong aside and touches me with his fingers, whispering with a knowing smile, "You're there."

He takes my hand and leads me into a room at the end of the hall. As we go past, the dreamlike image of Megan's cousin breaks into my consciousness. She's in a corner with a boy on top of her and seems to have hardly any clothes on. I smile at her, but she winces rather than smiles back, an uncertain look in her eyes. I'd like to help, make sure she's okay, but I can't, all I can do is cling to Ruben and concentrate on not tripping up in my heels.

We go into the room. I notice that it's nicely furnished with a double bed and a light on a bedside table. Ruben shuts the door and puts my bag on the bed. He opens it and pulls out the babydoll. He doesn't even have to ask. I put it on and let it slide over me. He helps me straighten it and kisses my neck, but when I lean over towards his mouth – it's so red right now, so unbelievable yet so real – he pulls away and says, "Wait, I'm not finished."

He ties the ribbons under my breasts then has me lie on the bed. He lies on top of me, I can feel his hands, his breath, and I start to moan.

"Good girl," he whispers. "You're ready."

He strokes my hips like he's sculpting my bottom, and pushes my legs slightly apart. "Bend your knees a bit, like this." I'm close to blacking out, and not just because of the pill that's rocking my brain from the core, making everything so vivid and perfect. The thought that Ruben will be inside me sweeps over me like a wave. I'm so excited I can hardly control myself.

"Now, Alek, listen," he whispers in my ear, caressing my chest. "Stay here, don't move, it'll all be okay. It'll

181

just take a few minutes then we'll be together all night. I promise you, we'll make love and wake up together in each other's arms."

I smile. It's what I've been waiting for. I nod and reach out to pull him closer. He pushes me away. "Not now. You just have to do this one thing for me first," he coaxes. His voice sounds so sweet, it wraps round my heart like honey, warming me. "You're beautiful. Relax, let yourself go, it'll be fun, you'll see."

Then he gets up and goes away.

My skin turns cold all of a sudden but there's no way I can get up and follow him and bring him back here, my legs still feel like they're somewhere else, disembodied, gone.

"Ruben," I mumble.

But Ruben's not in the room. There's someone else I don't know.

"Hi," he says.

I try to focus. It's a guy with greying hair, a bulky frame and a smell that makes me feel sick as soon as it hits me.

"Don't you remember me?" he asks, coming over.

I don't want him near me. I try to catch my breath and call out for Ruben but I can't. When the stranger's close enough to get a better look, I recognise him.

It's the guy from the building site.

I open my eyes wide in alarm but I can't move, everything's spinning so fast around me. I want to scream but my voice won't work. All I can muster is a whimper.

He stops speaking and looks at me while he undresses.

He does it slowly, seeming sure of the fact that I can't escape, that I won't put up a fight, that I won't say no the way I didn't say no the last time. Panic grips me. I don't understand what's happening. Rather, I do, but I can't work out how it all came about, why Ruben has gone away and isn't here to protect me like he always does. I shut my legs, the only physical action I can coordinate, and try to pull myself up on my elbows. The room starts to spin even faster so I have to lie down again.

The man drops his trousers to the floor. He's naked now, his socks the last thing he takes off. His loose and flabby flesh, with its mantle of white hair, is looming over me.

"I know it's your first time," he says, leaning on the bed, pulling at the ribbons on the babydoll. He sounds almost kind, but he still grabs hold of my knees and forces my legs apart. I let him, he's stronger than me, and I've no choice but to lie here, naked and defenceless. He groans and touches himself between his legs. "I won't hurt you. You're beautiful, you know. I would've paid whatever it took to have you."

He's touching me but he could just as easily have two hands round my neck, squeezing the air out of me, trying to kill me. I'd like to float out of my body and escape to the ceiling like I usually do, but I can't. I'm choking. I scrabble for air. I flail around trying to catch hold of something. My eyes hunt for Ruben's.

I hear the other man's voice. "Oh, yes," he says.

He spread-eagles me, his hands all over me, pushing and pulling at me like a rag doll. His mouth is slimy, he's devouring me, biting me, it hurts, I try to push against his shoulders to get him off but it's useless, he doesn't even notice. He just squeezes me tighter, he's grunting like an animal, using me like I'm not human.

I look at his body descending onto mine.

There is a scream and then darkness.

# 20

I run as fast as I can.

I tripped on the sheet and fell down the stairs, but I picked myself up and I'm out in the street now, running, trying to put as much distance as I can between me and that house, that room, that man.

The cold air revives me just enough, giving me the strength to decide where to go and keeping me on my feet even though I'm falling into a million pieces.

I'm naked, wrapped in a sheet, barefoot and running through the empty streets, hoping I don't bump into anyone, hoping no one sees me. I hide in a doorway when I hear a car. I'm crying. I can tell I'm crying because my face and neck are wet, not because I feel any actual emotions. The only thing driving me right now is panic.

Blurry-eyed, I flee, sobbing and feeling so wretched, so torn, that I contemplate lying down in the middle of the road and waiting for a car to hit me. But I keep on running until I turn into a familiar street that takes me to the entrance of the theatre. I push the door but it won't open. I go round the back of the building to the little door that opens with a key we keep under a plant pot.

I drop the key three times, and then my hands are shaking so much that getting the key in the keyhole is an impossible task. I finally manage it, and push the door open then slam it shut behind me while trying to catch my breath. I'm gulping for air and my lungs are hurting.

I slump on the ground, in a heap, pulling the sheet tight around me. I can hear music in the distance, like it's coming from a deep well, somewhere inside the theatre. I'm sobbing uncontrollably now, twisting the damp sheet in my fingers, too scared to move, afraid of everything.

I've no idea how long I lie here, unmoving.

A long shadow falls over me.

I look up in terror and through my tears I see Jonah.

He seems to be in his pyjamas. He's standing in the shadows, and I can't make out his face.

"G-go away," I mumble.

Without saying anything, he comes over, lifts me up and carries me in his arms down the corridor that leads to the stage. I keep crying and he mouths something to me – "Don't worry, it's going to be all right." His words make me sob even louder; I don't believe him.

He goes past the wings and heads to the very back of the theatre, skirting Helena's scenery then slipping through an opening in the wall. Behind it there's a room that smells of mould and damp. It contains a bed, a table and a sofa. In the corner is a gas stove with a wobbly blue flame.

He eases me onto the sofa, picks up a cover from the bed and lays it over me. Then he sits down beside me, not touching me, waiting for me to calm down. I'd rather not be here with him. I have no idea why he's here at this time of night and I had no idea this room existed, but I'm still sobbing too hard to talk or ask any questions. My heart is racing. I don't trust Jonah, I don't like Jonah, but his is a familiar face and I accept it. I don't have much choice. I don't know where else to go, I've got no one to ask for help.

"Shall I make you a hot drink?" he asks me when he realises I'll probably never calm down. Without waiting for me to reply, he gets up and switches on a travel kettle sitting on top of a tiny fridge. He sets out a cup, a teabag and some sugar, his movements hypnotising me so that the sobs at last begin to ease and the tears slide down in silence.

He hands me a cup of boiling hot tea and it's a relief to have something warm in my hands after the cold outside. I'm shivering, so I pull the cover tighter and take a shaky sip of my tea. It dawns on me now that the music is louder in here, and I notice it's coming from a stereo on the table. The tune helps to settle my head, as if the notes were nudging it back towards the right rhythm. The words, sung by a sweet, familiar female voice, lull me. As I let my back sink into the sofa I realise how rigidly I've been sitting, ready to run away again.

"Feeling better?"

I nod.

"What happened?"

"I killed a man."

It slips out on its own, effortlessly. The words had been going round and round in my head for so long that there was no hesitation; as soon as I opened my mouth they came out.

Of all the answers Jonah was expecting, this probably wasn't one of them. He stares at me, waiting for me to continue, but I can't speak.

"You killed a man," he repeats cautiously. "Okay. As a killer, that's quite a career you're building for yourself."

His sarcasm, in this room, in the middle of the night, has a different taste to it. This time it's like disinfectant. It burns and soothes at the same time.

"Did you hide the body before you came here?" he asks me, looking serious.

I burst into hysterical laughter. I can't help myself and some of the tea ends up on the cover.

He smiles for a second then turns serious again. "Tell me how I can help you. But you have to start from the beginning."

I can't face it. I can't get any more words out, the syllables are stuck deep inside of me and have no intention of getting themselves into the right order. I shut my eyes. I can see the scene; it's on an excruciating loop in my mind's eye. I was about to be raped. The stranger, the man with the grey hair, was on top of me, ignoring my tears and saying again and again, "It'll be over in a second. Just a second."

My mind was about to black out but a single thought kept flickering, like the light at the end of the tunnel – *this second will last for ever.*

I should say no.

All you have to do is say no, Megan had said.

"No," I rasped. "No."

But the man didn't listen, he was panting loudly, touching me, about to enter me.

"Be a good girl," he grunted. "Open your legs wide so it won't hurt."

I kept saying, again and again, "No, no, no."

But he opened them for me.

I reached over to the bedside table, stretching as far as I could, feeling around with my fingers until they touched the cold metal of the lamp. I grabbed it, ripped it out of the socket and smashed it over the man's head as hard as I could. He slumped onto me with one last groan, of pain not pleasure, staring at me for a second with shock vivid in his eyes.

His blood dripped onto my hands and over the bed as I struggled to free myself from the dead weight of his body. Grappling in a frenzy, disgusted, I slid out from under him and caught my breath. I was in a strange room, naked, and I'd killed a man.

I wrenched the sheet off the bed and quickly wrapped it round me. I opened the door to peep into the hall; it was empty and dark. The deafening music coming from the living room was enough to cover the strangled sobs I was struggling to stifle, even with a hand over my mouth.

I sneaked down the hallway in a sweat, praying no one would see me. As I passed a half-open door, I caught the fleeting sound of crying then Megan's voice, harsh. "It's no big deal, don't start acting like a baby now."

I hurried on, found the front door and bolted out. I fell down the stairs of the tower block, then made my way here. And now I don't know what to do.

"Fucking hell," Jonah says. I stare at him, amazed. "That's a bad story. We need to find a way of getting you out of this."

Did I just speak?

"Are you hurt?" he asks me. I don't know. I've got pains all over my body but I don't know if I'm hurt. "You need to check. Go into the bathroom, I'll wait for you here."

He gets up again and picks up a box with a red cross on it. "Everything you need's in here, but if you want a hand, give me a shout," he says. "Go through there, you know the way."

He points to the opening in the wall that we came through earlier. I take the box and limp to the bathroom. My right foot hurts but I can't face looking at it. In front of the mirror, I count the bruises and scratches that have appeared without my realising it. I wipe them with cotton wool dipped in antiseptic, and grit my teeth at the sting of it. It's like my body is finally telling me what it's been through, like it's just woken up in the worst possible way.

When I head back to Jonah, I notice that the opening to the secret room has always been there, behind Helena's scenery along the back wall, hidden by the rusty metal cabinet that Jonah keeps all his cables and tools in. The cabinet's been moved to the side now, like a door off its hinges.

"My f-foot h-hurts," I tell Jonah, hobbling over to him.

"Let me see," he says, and I sit back down on the sofa, exhausted. He lifts my foot up gently and whistles, not in a reassuring way. "There's a huge splinter in the sole of your foot and it's bleeding," he announces. "I need to get it out and it's not going to be nice."

"Okay," I mumble, shutting my eyes.

The pain is excruciating. I feel the wound piercing all the way to my heart and my head. I start crying again, as the thoughts come flooding back and my skin burns like it's been scalded.

"Listen, I'd like to give you a tetanus injection," Jonah adds after he's tended a bit more to my foot.

I open my eyes and see that he's bandaged it and I realise that it doesn't hurt as much. I stare at him, amazed again. He lowers his eyes and sighs. "Let's keep the explanations for another time," he says, heading off any questions I might have. "You can trust me, I'm an expert nurse."

"Eh, r-really?" I protest feebly. My eyes are shutting, but I have no intention of being a guinea pig for this madman in pyjamas. "And who have you nursed? The mice?"

I try to pull my foot out of his hands but he holds onto it. "I've nursed myself, okay?" he snaps. "I can take you to A&E if you'd rather."

He knows that's the last thing I want. I lie my head back, resting it on the arm of the sofa. "No. Y-you do it."

I don't feel the injection. The needle can't penetrate the thick wall of pain around my body. I watch Jonah work confidently and the questions start to mount up in my head.

He leaves the room and comes back not long after with some clothes from the wardrobe room. "You can't stay in that sheet, you'll freeze to death," he tells me.

He hands me some overalls that look enormous but warm. I take them and he turns away to give me time to put them on, but I can't. I'm finding it impossible to coordinate even the slightest of movements. I just want to sleep. So that's what I do. I shut my eyes.

"Are you done?" I hear in the distance. Then, "Okay. I'll give you a hand."

From the faraway place I've drifted to, I feel Jonah dressing me like I'm a two-year-old. He zips up the overalls, lifts me up and lays me on the bed. I'm absorbed into the heat of the chunky duvet, take one last hazy look at the flame in the stove, and I fall asleep, lulled by the music from the stereo.

# 21

Jonah's room has disappeared again.

He slid the cabinet back in front of the opening, then we went to get something to eat because I was starving and his fridge was practically empty.

When the others arrived after lunch, we behaved as normal, ignoring Electra's astonished gaze and her "Why are you wearing overalls?" question.

I got control of myself, one breath at a time.

Jonah keeps checking the news on his phone but there's no reports of middle-aged men turning up dead in the area. We reckon this means he might have got off with a bit of spilt blood and a sore head. It's a relief and a disappointment all at once, because underneath it all I'm angry. I know that mostly I'm angry with myself, but Jonah told me not to do anything rash, to think about what I want to do next and to stay away from the parties.

The first thing I'll do is try to understand it all. Which includes understanding why Jonah's been so good to me and why he seems different from the guy I usually can't stand. It's like he was wearing a mask before and now he's taken it off.

For now, though, I'm focusing my attention on rehearsals. Being Lady Hester gives me a chance to feel clean again. Her words are my words. Her love for Gerald is my love, for a few hours anyway. It feels so good that I give the performance of my life. Thomas is absolutely speechless. He's watching me, wide-eyed, as if he's scared to breathe.

I can see Jonah from the stage. He's in the wings, Helena beside him, sitting cross-legged on the floor. They're just the same. Jonah, with his blond hair, bandana, and that impossible sneer. Helena, dishevelled and beautiful, a sad, angry look in her eyes, and her scuffed combat boots on. Yet they look different to me.

I realise I'm back on board the Ship of Fools and that maybe this is where I belong. That there's nothing wrong with being different from normal people. But my immediate problem is trying to work out what's normal, and what's not.

My heart aches when I think of Ruben. I just can't explain it. I wonder what can have happened. Why on earth did he let that man come into the room? Why wasn't he there to protect me?

I feel betrayed.

After rehearsals, Jonah shuffles over. His hands are in the pockets of his tight, scruffy jeans. "You were amazing," he murmurs. I glimpse a sparkle in his eyes. "Do you want me to walk you home?"

I shake my head. "N-no, it's okay."

He smiles. "If you need anything, you know where to find me now."

I smile too and feel my jaw hurting. "Yes. In with the m-mice."

I make my way to the door, my heart swelling but not just with pain. I bump into Helena as I'm about to head over to the bus stop, and then I notice a familiar car at the side of the road, opposite the theatre.

I keep walking, head down, hoping he won't see me.

I don't want to see him.

But he starts the engine, burning rubber as the car screeches over, and he pulls up alongside me, lowering the window. I look around, desperate.

"Get in," Ruben hisses, his face hard.

I can see Helena unlocking her moped. She lifts her head and stares at me, from twenty metres or so down the street. I want to scream out to her, but Ruben puts the handbrake on and jumps out the car. He grabs my arm and drags me round to the passenger side then shoves me in violently, slamming the door.

I try to open it as he goes back round to the driver's side but it's blocked, he must've put the child lock on. I lower the window to shout something, anything, but Ruben grabs my hair and says, "Don't do it. Don't make things worse for yourself."

His voice sounds different. There's no trace of the gentle, patient Ruben. This is the voice of someone I don't know, and it terrifies me. He drives in silence, heading out of town in dead calm. But he's gripping the steering wheel so tight that his knuckles have gone white.

I try to think of a way out of this mess. I feel trapped. I don't know what he's capable of, now that he's so different.

He pulls into a clearing in the middle of nowhere, in front of a deserted building site.

"So, you think you're smart, do you, Aleksandra?" he asks me in a firm voice.

It sounds like a real question, one that he expects an answer to, but I don't know what to say, given that I'm the least smart person in the world and he for one should know that.

"We had an *agreement* and you broke it," he states. His complete calm crushes me. "All you had to do was let yourself go, for a minute, no more. But you smashed the guy's head in instead. You have no idea what I've had to do to keep him quiet."

I look down at my hands, the tears hot in my eyes. "Th-there w-was n-no a-a-g-g-g–"

"Agreement, you stupid cow," he shouts. "You can't even speak properly, what the fuck hope do you have in life? You should be grateful for our agreement, thankful that I gave you this opportunity."

I'm getting more and more confused. I don't know what he means and his insults shock me. I don't know how to react. This isn't the Ruben I'm in love with.

"And, for your information, there certainly was an agreement, even if you'd rather pretend there wasn't," he adds.

He pulls his phone out of his jacket, taps it a few times, then hands it to me, saying, "Enjoy the show. It might help jog your memory."

I take the phone, my hands shaking, and see there's a video playing on the screen. To begin with, I can't work out what it is, then the frame zooms in to show a girl. She's dancing, taking her clothes off in time to the music. She ends up topless, baring huge breasts that the camera lingers over. My ears burn as the girl turns her back and bends over to show her bottom and the narrow strip of fabric running through it. Hands reach out to touch her. The picture changes, the room changes, but the scene's more of the same. The same girl, still naked, now has her head bent between the legs of a fat man with his trousers down. There's a small crowd round her, urging her on as her head moves faster and faster, eliciting waves of applause and laughter. Then she's on a chair, masturbating, in someone's house, surrounded by people. Images of hands, mouths, bodies flash past, one after the other, until the scene switches to broad daylight. It looks like some kind of office, a man's on a swivel chair next to a desk and the girl with the huge breasts is between his legs while he moans and forces her head down.

Everything turns to a blur as a tear drops onto the screen, my hand trembling so much that Ruben grabs his phone back and stops the video.

"There's so much I could do with this," he tells me.

His voice sounds muffled to my ears, but it lacerates my frozen heart.

"And if you try to press charges, I will give evidence. I will show this in a court of law. The judge would see what you did willingly for my mate and would question why you're complaining when he wanted more of the same."

Ruben pauses then grabs me by the hair, forcing me to look him straight in the eye.

"Or maybe I'll post it online. Then everyone will know what you are and anything you say will be taken for what it is. The word of a whore. Do you get my drift?"

He yanks my hair, forcing me to nod.

"Now," he says, business-like. "You owe me money. A lot of money. For the clothes, the shoes, the dinners, and the fortune I lost last night because of you. You're going to pay it all back, or I'll make your life hell."

But they were all presents, I want to tell him. I never asked him for any of it. I never wanted a lacy black babydoll. I don't like high-heeled sandals. But it's too late. From the look on his face I realise the only thing that matters is that I accepted all those things. What I thought, what I think now, doesn't matter; only what I did matters. And he has that horrible video that will be remembered for ever.

"I th-thought that y-you ... that I ..." I try to say.

He sneers. "I know what you thought. What do you take me for, an idiot?" he says. "The perfect boyfriend who comes to pick you up and take you to the theatre. Reminds me of an old film. But even in that she was a whore, wasn't she? And this is my film. I decide how it ends."

A pathetic whimper comes out my mouth.

He smiles and puts the boot in. "Welcome to the real world, *girlfriend*. You're going to fuck whoever I say now, you'll take the money, you'll keep working the parties and keep doing what you were made for. After all, who else is going to want you now?"

He lets my head go and yanks at my overalls, pulling down the zip to expose my bare body.

"No one wants a whore as a girlfriend. Whores are for everyone."

I twist away and lash out at him. I don't want him to touch me but he grabs my wrists and stares at me, unflinching. I thrash about but can't get him off me until, all of a sudden, the driver's door is thrown open. Ruben turns round in shock only to receive a kick in the face. A kick from a heavy, scuffed combat boot.

"What the fuck ..." Ruben's hand shoots up to his face, trying to protect his nose, but blood pours through his fingers as he groans in pain.

Helena is standing by the driver's door.

Trembling and confused, I gather my wits and wind down the window, squeeze my hand through and open the door from the other side. I scramble out, fall on my knees in the dust, get back up.

Ruben is about to come after me but Helena raises her arm, a knife clenched in her hand.

"I'll kill you," she warns him, serious and self-assured. Her voice is as sharp as the blade in her hand, promising to do exactly what she's just said. She's not kidding, I've no doubt about it. It's the first time I've heard her speak in all the time I've known her. I can't take my eyes off her angry face as it pins Ruben to his seat.

"Okay, okay, keep your hair on," he says, moving his hands slowly onto the steering wheel. "I'm not moving, see?"

His face is caked in blood and in a flash I see him for what he is, a horrible person hiding behind a perfect face.

Helena issues one last warning. "Keep away from her," she tells him, her voice rough like gravel.

Then she takes her knife and drags it along the side of Ruben's car. She presses so hard you can hear the metal screech.

"Shit, stop!" Ruben shouts. "Not my car!"

Helena kicks the door shut. "Fuck you."

She walks away, heading towards the moped parked down the street. I follow her, shocked, tripping over myself. She sits down, leaving space for me on the seat so I can get on behind her. I hold on tight and feel her fragile body in my arms.

"Th-thanks," I say.

She doesn't reply, just accelerates and pulls away. As we speed along, I'm amazed by how much can be said with the turn of a wrist on an accelerator handle.

# 22

Helena drops me at the gate, nods and then takes off without a word.

I'd like to say thanks but I realise that I don't have to. I realise she already knows, maybe she's always known about everything, even before I did.

As soon as she rides off, I head over to Megan's.

Carla comes to the door but when she sees me in overalls, hair all over the place from a night sleeping rough and my face a mess after what I've been through in the past 24 hours, she scowls and very subtly, so as not to be noticed, tries to close the door again.

"What do you want?" she asks abruptly.

"Is M-Megan in?" I ask, looking her straight in the eye.

"Yes, but she's studying and I'd rather you didn't bother her, given that it doesn't happen that often," she replies, keeping the door more shut than open.

I sigh. I am familiar with Megan's study afternoons and I know I won't be interrupting anything intellectual. But I can't tell her mum that, so instead I insist, "It won't take long. I just need to ask her something urgent."

She hesitates. "Listen, I'm going to come straight to the point. You're my best friend's daughter and I'm sorry you're having a hard time right now, but I want you to stop dragging Megan into it."

I look at her, puzzled.

It must show on my face, because she says, "Don't pretend you don't understand. I know what you're up to and I only hope your mum finds out too, sooner or later."

Then she hisses, "Just leave my little girl out of it. Tell her what you have to then don't come back. Is that clear?"

I sense that whatever this woman thinks she knows is a distorted version of the truth, but I don't have the time or the energy to argue with her. I nod and limp along beside her, ignoring her accusing look.

I knock on Megan's door and when she doesn't answer, I go in anyway. She's lying on the bed, face down, but when I go over, I notice her eyes are wide open, staring into space.

"You're here," she says. Even her voice sounds different, tired, harsh, not friendly at all. I stand there twiddling my thumbs, unsure how to begin. There's a smell of booze in the air which means Megan must have been drinking and won't be very sober, but I need to speak to her anyway.

"I thought you were my friend," I begin, lamely. It's not the best start but it's what comes out on impulse.

Megan sits up, leaning on one elbow, her back against the headboard. "We are friends," she replies, narrowing her eyes. "I shared everything with you, my world, my friends. You made loads of money thanks to me."

"But you w-weren't honest with me," I insist, wavering. "Y-you could've t-told me how things r-really were. I d-didn't know what I w-was doing."

She shrugs and looks at me, contempt in her eyes. "You knew fine well, we all know from day one," she hisses. "It's just easier to pretend it's something else, isn't it?"

She pouts, shuts her eyes and mimes a kiss, imitating my voice, "Oh Ruben, my darling! I l-love you so much I w-want to be your whore."

She cackles so cruelly it sends shivers down my spine.

"Why d-did you d-do it?" I ask, clenching my fists. "I got the money. What was in it for you?"

She stops laughing and rolls her eyes skywards. "Do you know why it's so easy with girls like you? Because you're nice. You're not a slut like Dani; she'd stab you in the back soon as look at you. And you're not trying to act big like my cousin. No, you're just used to being told how to behave. You're so worried about what people think of you that you're incapable of saying no."

I lower my eyes, hurt.

"I'll prove I'm your friend," she cries, jumping off the bed to stand in front of me. "I'll answer your question. You need to know that for every pound you earned, Ruben made two. Young girls like you don't come cheap, you know. Not for the men who buy them."

I know that this too is said to hurt me.

"Never mind him. What about you?" I ask, looking her in the eye. "Why d-did you d-drag me into it?"

"You girls are mine," she replies, proudly. "I decide

who's in and who's out. Every month I get a bonus for each of you. If you can call it that."

I sit down on the bed.

The room's spinning and it's not spinning because I've been drinking. It's spinning because of my stupidity. My naivety. My desire not to see what had been staring me in the face from the start.

"B-but why m-me?"

Why pick a clown like me? Some insecure blob with no friends and no experience? Why invest so much time and money in me, when Megan could have easily found far less inhibited girls?

"Because you're a virgin," she says.

I don't understand. I shake my head, mortified, aware that nothing and nobody will ever be able to delete what brought me to where I am now, this room, this conversation.

"A sixteen-year-old virgin is a rare species," she says, sniggering, laughing like it's hilarious until she sees how bewildered I am. "You just don't get it, do you? A virgin is worth loads, there are men who'll pay ridiculous amounts of money to be the first one to fuck her," she explains, sitting down beside me. "I sold my virginity for £1,500 when I was fourteen. It could have been more, but my tits aren't as big as yours. I told you – men are idiots."

Every single word she says is awful. I wish she'd stop. I put my hands over my ears but she tickles me to get me to take them off, like I'm a little girl.

"No, you have to listen," she says softly. "Don't ruin

everything. The business only lasts a couple of years; they want them younger and younger out there. But if you're clever, if you play your cards right, you'll be able to save enough money to go to university, buy a car, whatever you want."

"I d-don't care," I reply, between sobs. "I th-thought Ruben l-liked me. That was the only th-thing that mattered."

Megan strokes my hair and her touch is surprisingly soothing. "You see? You're a nice girl," she tells me. "When I told my mum you'd asked me to sell myself, I had a hard time making her believe it."

"What?" I exclaim, alarmed. "That's n-not true! It w-was you!"

"I know. But she started stressing me and asking all these questions, so I turned it round and made out you were to blame. Now all she wants is that I stay away from you," she says, as natural as anything. "We just have to pretend not to see each other for a while then she'll forget all about it."

I pull away from her and jump up from the bed, furious.

"I'll t-tell the p-police," I scream, flipping out now. "You'll all pay for what you're doing."

"You won't be telling anyone," she states, crossing her legs. "If I were you, I'd be more concerned about that video."

I look at her and I'm shaking with rage and pain. Tears slide down my cheeks, beyond my control. I don't want

to cry in front of Megan, but I can't stop. I'm trapped.
They played with me like a doll, a toy, an object, and I let
them. It looks like there's no escaping them.

"If I were you," she continues, "I'd be scared of Ruben
too. His back's well covered, his parents are big fish.
You're going to have to do what he wants or they'll
destroy you."

Her words slide past me. My life's not worth living
anyway.

But my brain keeps working overtime, trying to find a
way out. It keeps hitting one dead end after another, like
flies slamming blindly into a window. But it won't give
up, it keeps searching.

Next I try to reason with Megan. She's a bright girl, not
stupid at all, and I can't believe she doesn't realise how
monstrous this whole situation is.

"W-we can g-get out t-together," I tell her. "You're
g-good at m-making clothes, there are other th-things you
c-can d-do for a living."

"Why should I?" she replies, lying back on the bed
now with her arms behind her head. "I make more in
one night than some people make in two weeks in their
crappy jobs," she says. "I get to have fun, spend time with
my friends and have all the sex I want."

I refuse to think she actually believes what she's
saying. It's like she's playing a part, from her voice it
sounds like she's reciting something she's learned off by
heart to stop herself from drowning. I can see my own
lies in hers. When the world gets twisted and threatens to

swallow you up, all you can do is tell yourself stories to make it seem better than it is.

"I-it's not f-fun and y-you know it," I hit back.

She gives me the finger. "Boys expect you to have sex. They're always asking for it," she says. "So why not make them pay for something that you'll end up having to do anyway?"

"And what d-does L-Lee think of y-you?" I ask, looking for the right button to press. Trying to make the last few pieces of the puzzle fit into place.

"Lee is fine with things the way they are. We're a modern couple," she answers breezily. She raises her hand to show me the ring she never takes off. "You would've loved one from Ruben, wouldn't you?" she crows, making my blood run cold.

Then she waves me away, her ring glinting. "I've got a headache," she says, as she lies back down on the bed. "Get over it. A quick fuck's no big deal, you'll get used to it. And we'll still be friends."

I turn, and I'm heading for the door when I hear her voice again.

"You're on your own, Alek. No one wants out. If you try anything, you'll have them all against you. And I'll make you pay. That's a promise."

I'm on my own.

My own.

I say it to myself over and over as I drag myself home.

Then, when I get there, I open the door and see Ruben sitting on the sofa reading Matt a story.

# 23

A family dinner.

My mum's idea. "We never see each other, even though we live in the same house," she tells Ruben as she sets the table.

He's sitting up straight on the sofa, holding Matt on his knee. He doesn't seem bothered that Matt is pulling his hair and putting his sweaty little hands all over his bandaged face. He looks like he's enjoying it.

"Oh, my parents are always out at work too," he replies politely. He doesn't look at me, letting me stand here in absolute panic, unable to react.

My mum notices.

"Alek, you look tired," she says. "Is something the matter?"

Ruben pulls his mobile out of his pocket, as if he needs to check his messages, but I know it's meant as a warning for me.

"R-rehearsals," I manage to stammer. "They were really h-hard."

"Why not have a shower while I finish getting the

dinner ready?" she suggests. "Luke will be back in half an hour, and I've asked Ruben to stay for dinner, since he's been here a while, waiting for you."

Ruben's expression is unfathomable. The plaster across his nose is distorting his face, giving him an almost diabolic look. I can see that he has no intention of declining my mum's invitation; if anything, he seems to have come with the specific intention of forcing his way into this one last part of my warped life. It doesn't take me long to work it out. If his car had been parked outside I would never have come in, so he must've left it down a side street on purpose. He's here to drop me in it, to get me back for his broken nose. And for everything else, too.

I go into the bathroom to buy some time.

As the jet of hot water runs through my hair and down my body, I rack my brains for an idea. I think about climbing out the window, ringing Jonah, but none of them will draw this nightmare to a close.

Ruben will hunt me down until I pay him back everything I owe him.

My tears flow into the scalding water, but I promise myself they'll be the last. I have no right to cry, no right to feel sorry for myself. I get dried and put my clothes on, digging out one of my old flannel shirts and a baggy pair of jeans from the wardrobe. I sit down at the table, stiff, nervous. The others don't notice me, they're too busy chatting.

"Ruben broke his nose playing golf," my mum tells her

husband, who has just arrived home. "I never knew it was one of those extreme sports ..."

They all laugh.

Ruben reaches across the table and takes my hand, as smooth as can be. He squeezes it and cold creeps across my skin. I don't dare pull away. I don't dare speak.

"I'd like to take Aleksandra to my house by the beach this weekend, if you're happy for her to come with me," he says.

He's so good at playing the part of the ideal boyfriend. The kind every parent would love for their daughters. He's polite, handsome, sophisticated. He looks at them with bright, confident eyes, like those of an adult. He's winning their trust with every clear syllable he speaks.

I want to scream "NO!" as loud as I can, with every last scrap of breath in my body. But I don't. I sit there, immobile, my hand stuck in his. I listen to my mum saying, "Well, that is kind of you, Ruben. I don't see a problem with that."

Then Luke clears his throat. "I'm not sure," he says. "All these nights away, Aleksandra's a bit young."

He looks at me.

I see him for the first time. I'd like to tell him he's right. I'd like to tell him, yes, I am just a young girl, but the adult world is sucking me in and I didn't expect it to be so cruel.

Ruben squeezes my fingers imperceptibly in his. "I promise it'll be the last time," he says in an understanding voice. "It's my birthday, actually, and I wanted to celebrate it with a few friends. My parents eventually agreed after a lot of debate. In fact, they only gave in with the proviso they can hire a couple of bouncers for the night. To make sure nothing untoward happens."

Luke is watching him.

Ruben keeps smiling. "But I don't want to insist, sorry. You're in charge –"

"Oh come on, Luke, don't go all strict on us now," my mum interrupts, passing the dish of roast beef around. "If Aleksandra wants to, we can let her go just this once, don't you think? It's her boyfriend's birthday."

Luke looks down at his plate and mumbles, "Okay then. It's not for me to be a spoilsport."

Ruben lets go of my hand and starts eating, slicing into the meat.

"The th-thing is, this weekend, I've got the d-dress r-rehearsal at the theatre," I manage to say. "I d-don't think I'll b-be able to c-come."

"Oh, I didn't know that," Ruben says, and he honestly looks like a crestfallen but considerate boyfriend. He kicks my leg under the table. Then he pulls out his phone and swipes it a few times. "Mrs Ramelli, I'd like to show you something I'm sure you'll like."

He hands his phone over to my mum.

She reaches out, smiling and chewing on her dinner, no idea that her world is about to fall apart. Horrified, I watch the scene play out in slow motion, the device passing in front of me, then I take a deep breath and I'm about to shout, "I can sort it. I'll tell Thomas I have to leave early on Saturday."

But it's too late. The phone has reached the other side of the table. My mum looks at the screen, smiling.

Then she cries out, "Oh my God! Who is it?"

Sweat's pouring down me. I think I'm going to die.

"I ... I ..." I try to say.

"My sister," Ruben replies proudly, interrupting me. "She's four. It took my parents a while to realise it's hard being an only child sometimes."

"She's so sweet," my mum comments before giving Ruben his phone back. I gag on the ball of fear that has solidified in my stomach, making me feel like throwing up.

Ruben puts his phone down between us, reminding me what I can expect if I don't do as I'm told. He's at ease, friendly, carrying on the conversation in a way that makes even Luke start to relax and laugh at his clever jokes.

I'm in bits by the time the meal's over.

My mum lets us go to my room before Ruben has to leave. She thinks she's doing me a favour, but she's actually forcing me to be alone with him.

He sits on my bed. I stay by the closed door, even though I know it would be pointless to run away.

"The scratch your friend made on my car will cost two grand to repair. Plus a grand for the broken nose," he begins, coldly. "So, your first fuck won't earn you anything as you'll be giving every penny of it to me."

His words are a prison sentence.

It doesn't occur to him that I might refuse, and he's right. He's used to winning, people like him always win.

But I promised myself I wouldn't cry. I gather myself together, imagine the stage, the lights, the audience.

Jonah backstage, shining the spotlight on me.

"Okay," I say, keeping my voice low. "You're right. I'm sorry about everything that happened, I was out of my head. But I talked to Megan earlier, and I know I made a mistake."

I sound convinced and convincing. But still he studies me, dubious. I guess he thought he'd have to insist more.

"Three grand for the weekend," he stresses, "plus four for past expenses. You should be able to do it in a month. After that you can keep whatever you make."

I nod.

"But I want to find the client myself, for the weekend," I add. I realise I'm not stuttering, absorbed in the role I'm playing, so I try to make it more real. "T-to pay you b-back for the m-mess last n-night."

His eyes don't leave mine, he doesn't trust me. "I hope you're not trying to pull a fast one, Alek."

"No, no tricks," I state confidently, even though my heart's on fire.

But he doesn't let it go; he's playing it safe.

"Prove it."

I know what he means even before he unbuttons his trousers.

"I want to see if you still love me," he adds, calling me out. "Come over here and prove it."

If I don't, he'll know I'm bluffing.

I move closer, swallowing my pride and the pure humiliation, as I stand before him for the first time ever with a clear head. I've had no alcohol, no drugs. The harsh reality is laid bare in the light of the bulb hanging from the ceiling. I manage a smile.

"Take your clothes off."

I hesitate. "The d-door doesn't l-lock," I tell him.

"Take your clothes off," he repeats. "Your mum won't come in. She seemed to want to leave us alone for a while." He sniggers; he's been playing with her as well as me. I have no choice but to undress, promising myself this will be the last time someone forces me or talks me into it.

I reach out to switch off the light, but he shakes his head. "I want to look at you. You're the fittest whore I've got. I get the privilege of having you all to myself whenever I want." I walk over to him, forcing myself to sway my hips and look self-assured and relaxed. "Because that's the way it's going to be, you know. Everyone else will pay, but you'll always give it to me free."

The world stops.

The silence is deafening.

As I bend over him, I can hear every noise, see every detail. I fight the urge to retch, and I do what's expected of me. He's not kind this time. He doesn't bother to check that I feel okay with it, or that I at least think I'm okay with it. He simply grabs my hair and pushes me down, touching me and saying "whore" over and over.

I wonder how long it will take to fill the empty space that word is gouging out inside me. I wonder if I'll ever manage to think I'm anything else. It's so easy to believe him. *Whore*. That's what I am right now. It's what I've been, in all the weeks I've been with him.

I fly up to the ceiling for what I hope is the last time.

I look down at myself and ask, *Who are you?*

I look at Ruben who's using me as if I'm a nobody, a creature with no name, no heart, no soul. Just an empty body.

When he's finished, he lies down on the bed and pulls out a pack of cigarettes. I didn't know he smoked – he's never smoked in front of me before. He lights one, closes his eyes and takes a long, satisfied drag. He hasn't even bothered to pull up his trousers.

I stay on the floor, daring only to pick up my shirt and put it on slowly, then button it one at a time.

"Well done, Alek. You blow me away," Ruben says, after two more drags on the cigarette. "It's going to be perfect between us. You won't want for anything; you'll be safe with me as long as you do what you're told. What do you think?"

"O-okay," I reply from the hollow depths of despair I've sunk to.

He laughs and looks at me like I'm stupid. "It'll have to be okay," he says, enjoying himself. "You don't have any choice."

# 24

I smear on layers of make-up to conceal the shadows
under my eyes.

There are seven of us in the dressing room, plus Helena
who's curled up in a lopsided armchair, watching us like a
scientist collecting data.

I can see her reflection in the mirror. I look closer at
my own image, pale and caked in make-up thick enough
to mask every flaw except the scars on my soul. Then I try
to focus on hers, dark against the faded fabric of the chair,
her big eyes, her tool belt lying beside her.

She's a ball of supressed anger.

After what she did to Ruben, the ruthless way she
put a knife to his face, I know there has to be something
torturing her inside.

I wait for the other *grandes dames* to go out, ready for
the dress rehearsal. Hester doesn't go on right away, so I
can afford to linger for a few more minutes.

"Did you h-hide that n-note in my p-pocket?" I ask
her without turning round. I pull on the tatty-looking
wig with blond ringlets that Electra gave me as part of my

costume. While I fix it in place with hairpins, I see Helena nodding out of the corner of my eye.

"H-how did you know?" I persist.

She doesn't answer. She would have to put it into words and I appreciate she doesn't want to, that it could be some time before I get another chance to hear the voice she used yesterday.

"Well, I w-wanted to s-say thanks anyway," I tell her, turning to face her not her reflection. "It d-didn't solve the problem, but it's given me time to f-find a solution."

In response, she pulls the hammer out of her belt and hands it to me. I think she means, "Strike back."

I nod.

"D-do you think," I continue, "I c-can trust J-Jonah?"

I don't know why I'm asking her, maybe it's because she seems to understand people just by looking at them. Because she didn't presume it was just a lovers' tiff between me and Ruben, she followed us, she knew what was happening.

Helena nods three times, deadly serious. Then she gestures with her hands, clasping them together as if to say, "Good friend."

I remember seeing them talking together, or rather, Jonah talking while she listened, a few days after her hammering fit.

I start to think that this theatre, this Ship of Fools, is hiding more secrets than I ever realised.

"I h-have to go," I say in the end. I go over to her chair and hold out my hand. She squeezes it and we smile.

Right now I feel brave, shored up by my plan, which I think is not actually that bad.

On stage, with our costumes on, the lights shining and the scenery in place, we get a preview of what it will be like in a few days' time. Even if the props have seen better days and our grand dresses are all patched up, I know the audience won't notice any of it. They'll be swept away by the magic of the performance, as if Oscar Wilde had come back to life for a few hours. That's what we're here for.

I use one of the times I'm not on stage to seek out Jonah in the wings.

"How's things?" he asks me with a smile that seems less of a sneer than usual.

"Fine," I reply. And then, after a pause, "I'd like to ask you something."

"I'm listening."

I am struck by the significance of this short statement, but all I say is, "A-after rehearsals."

"That means dinner then. At the best restaurant in town."

I go back onstage with a smile on my face. It's just as well that Lady Hester is supposed to be happy in this scene.

Later, we all leave the theatre together. I head to the bus stop and Jonah does his usual lap around the block, only this time I know what's going on.

As soon as the coast is clear, we meet at the back entrance of the theatre.

"Where are w-we g-going?" I ask.

"Here."

"Y-you said w-we were g-going to d-dinner," I say. "Are y-you g-going to roast some m-mice or something?"

"I think Oscar Wilde is getting to you," he comments, opening the door with the secret key. "You're getting far too sarcastic."

We go in and he tells me to wait a few minutes in the dressing room, just to give him time to check the table booking and arrange everything for the meal, champagne, caviar and all that stuff.

I start to laugh. He's still a bit weird, but I'm starting to decipher what he says without getting so worked up about it.

When he calls me, all the lights are off. Just a dim glow from the stage remains, casting a glimmer backstage, and I head in that direction.

Mrs Arbuthnot's drawing room is just the way we left it a few minutes ago. Only the table in the middle has been set for two with a candelabra twinkling in the centre, the fake silver one we used in *Phantom of the Opera*.

I call out "Jonah" and edge forward a few steps. A light comes on and a thousand drops of light dance around me in a snow effect, like blue-white fireflies. I smile and instinctively reach out to catch one of the snowflakes, as if they were real and I could grasp one.

"Please take a seat," I hear him proclaim. "Your waiter will be with you shortly."

I sit down at the table and smile as I wait. A song I

know starts to play, one of those ones Jonah's always listening to and that I've grown to love; it strikes a familiar chord inside me.

Then he appears, dressed as a waiter in a uniform that's too short, the cuffs of the shirt nearly at his elbows and the trousers only just reaching his ankles. "Don't say anything, it's the latest fashion," he declares, placing the tray he's carrying in the centre of the table. He pulls out a bottle of fizzy orange from his pocket, opens it and puts it next to the tray.

"*Et voilà*, Madame is served," he announces with an awkward bow. "And the waiter too," he adds, sitting down on the other chair.

We help ourselves to the cold meats and tinned vegetables he's arranged artistically, as if they were delicacies like lobster and crayfish. We don't speak to start with; I think we both feel embarrassed. We hardly know each other. We've never been alone in the same place for more than ten seconds without insulting each other or playing some silly prank.

"This m-music is b-beautiful," I say at last.

"Well, let's just say you can only hear it here," he says. He's taken off his bandana and tied his hair in a ponytail, revealing his face.

"W-why? Isn't it f-famous?"

"It's mine."

"What is?"

"The music, I wrote it," he replies, his eyes never leaving his plate. He seems uncomfortable talking about

220

it. He coughs. "You know all those buttons that annoy you so much? Well, you can create wonderful things with them."

"I d-didn't know you p-played," I say, aware that my mouth is hanging open.

"Oh, I thought you did, seeing as you stole that CD with the demos of my new songs," he replies, raising an eyebrow.

"I th-threw it away," I admit. "I w-wanted to g-get you b-back."

He sighs and shakes his head. "I need a new laptop and the synth I use drives me mad, but I'm not a bad electronic musician and have got some talent as a guitarist. And I didn't say that. Someone else did." He goes quiet when he sees my puzzled face. "Forget it. You wanted to ask me something."

There are so many questions I'd like to ask him but for now there's no time. I pull an envelope out of my bag, open it and place a pile of crumpled banknotes, tied together with a yellow elastic band, on the table.

"There's three thousand pounds in here."

"Oh, Madame, are you propositioning me? I cost a lot more than that, babes," he cries, raising his hands.

We burst out laughing. There's not much to laugh about, but it helps all the same. Then I tell him my plan. He has to come with me to the party on Saturday, buy my virginity and pay Ruben with the money I've earned over the past few weeks. Money that I've never touched until now.

"We'll go into a room for a few minutes then it'll be over."

"Okay." He nods. "It sounds like an excellent plan. But I do think you need something more conclusive. That guy won't stop hassling you, he'll never let you just leave."

"He h-has a v-video," I explain, hanging my head.

Then I tell him what happened yesterday and what Helena did.

"I know," he says. "She told me."

I stare at him, confused. "She s-speaks to y-you?" I ask.

"No. We've been messaging each other for a while," he admits. He looks up. "What? Are you surprised? You're the one who hasn't had time for anyone else in here."

His words hit home. I'd thought he was the one who only cared about himself.

"Helena asked me to tell you her story," he continues. "But I said it would be better if she did it herself, that maybe she could write you a letter. She loves writing as much as she hates speaking."

I'm curious. "Is it s-something to d-do with my s-situation?"

"Yes. And it didn't work out well for her," he answers. He pours some fizzy orange into a fake crystal glass. "Shall we get back to our problem?"

I like that he calls it ours.

He gets up before I can answer, goes off stage then comes back with something tiny in his hand. "It's a bug that I can hide in the pocket of my jacket. A friend can lend me a camera to hide in the same way. Let's fight your

222

demon prince with his own weapons. We'll make a nice home video of him, show everything he gets up to."

It seems a great idea. But I'm still afraid of how Ruben will react.

"If h-he f-finds out –" I start.

"He won't," Jonah interrupts. "We'll send the film to the police – anonymously."

He wobbles a bit over the last part. We both know that sending it anonymously won't protect me, that Ruben will still work out who's behind it.

"You have to give it a try," he insists. "You have to get out *and* destroy him. Just think how many other girls will fall into his trap if you don't stop him." He pauses, before adding, "If you don't act now, everything you've gone through will have been for nothing."

I can feel the sting of tears welling up but I try to force them back. "D-do you think that it all h-happened to me for a r-r-r ...?"

"A reason, of course there's a reason," he says. "Everything happens for a reason. What counts is how we react, how we deal with the things life throws at us."

He comes closer and puts his hands on my shoulders.

"That cow claiming to be your friend told you the same thing, didn't she? You're a nice girl," he adds. "That's why it happened to you. So you can save someone else."

Instinctively, I get up and hug him. We hold each other tight amid the snowflakes falling brightly around us, and I feel his words weaving a protective veil around me. They cover and clothe me, so that I'm not facing the world naked and alone.

"You can do it, Aleksandra," he tells me. It's the first time I've ever heard him say my name. "And even if it doesn't work out, at least you know you're not alone. I'm here, and there's Helena too. And other people you haven't realised yet."

I'm not alone.

I'm not alone.

With these words bold in my heart, I go home not long after, staring at the stars as I walk, looking up and not down at my feet. I think about Oscar Wilde and his play, about how many of history's greatest people also hide the greatest wounds. And how the strength they found to face their pain was perhaps what made them so great.

# 25

It turned out that the perfect plan needed some organising, mainly because Jonah doesn't have a car and Ruben's beach house where the party is being held is miles away.

So Jonah asked Thomas for a loan of his, allegedly to take a few things to the recording studio. Thomas was all right about it but Electra wasn't. She gave him the third degree, wanting to know all the ins and outs, like where, when and why? She also said, "You and Aleksandra have stopped fighting. Something's up."

In the end she gave in, sighing and waving in a way that could have meant either *good luck* or *bugger off*.

As planned, Ruben came by to pick me up, and there were two new girls in the car who I'd never seen before, two blonde girls, maybe sisters, who were holding hands in the back seat and giggling, probably drunk or high on something. I sat next to them because there was an older boy in the front playing a game on his phone with the volume up loud, driving me mad.

I was on edge. Looking at the two sisters, I realised

for the umpteenth time how stupid I'd been. It was impossible not to see what was going on from their clothes, their make-up, their shoes. Until a few days ago, I'd been dressing the exact same way, wearing the exact same make-up, and ignoring the truth of what I'd got myself into.

I looked at them and couldn't help but admire Megan's and Ruben's skill at making it all seem so cool, so normal, so much fun, while nudging you over an abyss, telling you it's what you've always wanted. Money, male attention, crazy parties, the kind of glittering future plenty of young girls find hard to resist. It's difficult to say no, because no means you're out, you're not part of the gang and you have to go back to a life that you don't want any more. And when you seduce someone, when you think you've seduced someone, all of a sudden you're no longer invisible, you feel wanted, and that's the only thing that counts. Existing, being visible, pleasing. Pleasing others, that is, because what happens to your own pleasure is a different story.

When I stop thinking about all this, I see we've arrived. I've bitten a fingernail to the quick, and only now I realise it stings like anything.

Once we're inside, at the party, I have to behave as normal while I wait for Jonah to show up. Megan arrives with Lee; she has a bruise on her neck but says it's a love bite her fiancé gave her. She's buzzing, organising the girls, and I notice straight away that she's keeping an eye on me. So I do what I can to reassure her, because she's smart and Jonah has no idea what to expect. I need to set the stage for him.

I grit my teeth and do the best strip of my life, thinking how it'll be my last one. Sober, it all looks so different. This world isn't colourful and bright, it's dark, seedy and stale. The girls dance without any real feeling, imitating moves they've seen on TV or in music videos. They're performing for the crowds of boys and men who can't get enough of them. Sweaty men, boys in trainers, all spaced-out on alcohol or drugs, looking at them in the same blank way they'd watch something on a screen, remote and detached; their only concern is to have some fun, kill some time in a way that asks nothing of them, then get back to their real lives.

Jonah turns up eventually. I pray with all my heart that he'll be okay when he sees me like this, half naked and provocative. He doesn't look around, but immediately approaches one of the bouncers, who points to Ruben in the corner.

He goes over to him and I notice he's well dressed, hair in a ponytail, freshly shaven and respectable. He moves with confidence, no hesitation; I can tell he's studied the part.

He mutters something to Ruben who smiles, shakes hands with him and points at me.

Jonah looks over, makes some comment that I can't hear and Ruben laughs. Then I see money changing hands, something I'd never noticed before. Ruben counts the notes and slips them into his pocket with a smile, then gives Jonah a friendly slap on the back. I watch his mouth spell out, "She's all yours. Enjoy."

The strip ends and the two of them come over, Ruben in front, Jonah behind him. All of a sudden, being naked from the waist up in front of someone from my other life embarrasses me, but I shut down the instinct that tells me to put my arms across my chest.

"You two know each other already," Ruben begins. "So I don't have to introduce you."

"Yes, that's right," Jonah responds. "We met online, actually. And she told me about these amazing men-only parties."

"Well, there are plenty of girls here too," Ruben scoffs, winking at Jonah. "But maybe not quite what you'd call girlfriend material."

They both laugh and I can hear from Jonah's forced chuckle that if we stay here a minute longer, he'll smack Ruben in the face.

I take him by the wrist and give him a coy, seductive look, sticking my chest out. "So, a-are you ready?" I ask him.

"I certainly am," he says, exhaling loudly. He's getting wound up, we need to move quickly.

"Just a sec," Ruben says. He pulls a pill out of his pocket and hands it to me. "Alek should take this. It'll loosen her up and make sure she gives it her all."

I take it between two fingers and notice that Ruben is watching to see if I swallow it, so I stick it in my mouth then put my arm round Jonah's waist and move him towards an empty room.

"I can't believe this place," he hisses.

"Shut up and follow me."

I spit the pill out into my hand.

We walk past loads of girls, all of whom are having sex, everywhere you look and in every way possible. I see Megan unbutton the trousers of a guy who's not even looking at her, he's too busy looking at his phone, sending a message. "I hope you're having fun," I tell her silently.

We shut ourselves in the room. We're safe, for now at least.

"H-have you f-filmed everything?"

"Oh yes," Jonah responds. "You should hear what he just said, that guy. I wanted to smash his face in, you know?"

"Yes, I noticed," I murmur. I pick a blanket up from a chair and pull it round me. "Let's sit down on the b-bed for now, but we should mess the sheets up a b-bit, stain them with s-something, so no one will s-suspect anything. Ten m-minutes then we can go out."

"Is that all these wankers last for?" Jonah asks sarcastically. "That'll be why they have to pay for it."

"Will you stop that, p-please?" I hiss. "We need to b-be quiet, if they c-catch us we're in t-trouble. Give me a h-hand instead of passing comment on everything."

The truth is I'm angry because he's seeing me how I would never have wanted him to see me. His sarcasm makes me feel even more stupid.

"What I don't understand," Jonah continues as he spits

on the sheets to wet them and I roll my eyes, "is how you ended up here in the first place. You're not like this."

I sigh. "None of these girls are like this. You end up doing stupid things just to feel wanted, to be part of something ... or at least not to feel so rejected," I tell him.

"Who cares if someone rejects you?" he says, grimacing. "The whole world doesn't have to love you, you know. Not like this anyway!"

I look at him. "Men fall for it too," I fire back. "They know they've got it easy with us, they just pay and don't have to pretend to be something they're not. They're afraid of being rejected too, in the real world. Here they hide behind their money."

He falls silent and seems to be mulling over what I've just said. I think how I have no idea when I worked all that out.

We sit side by side on the rumpled bed, checking the clock. Jonah takes my hand. "I'm really sorry," he murmurs.

"Me too," I say, feeling wretched. "But it's nobody's fault but mine."

"That's not true," he says. "Taking advantage of other people's vulnerability is wrong. And they gave you drugs."

But we'll never know who's really guilty; there are no good guys and bad guys in all this. I can see that now. We're all victims, all executioners, that's what bothers me. Ruben deceived me, but I let him. I didn't say no when I could have because I cared more about his reaction to me than my own feelings. I believed that sex was a game and you learn the rules by doing it, and only now I see that the only rule I should have been learning was to have some respect for myself.

"Mess up your clothes a bit," I tell Jonah before we leave the room. "Look sweaty, a bit pleased with yourself. As soon as we're out, I'll go to the bathroom and you go back to Ruben. Don't rush, film the party, hang around and chat with people if you can."

I open the door and am about to go when Jonah pulls me back and strokes my cheek. He stares at me for a second and I can see understanding, affection and support in his eyes. I'd like to say something but there are no words, so I just smile.

When I turn back round, Megan's in front of me, her eyeliner smudged and a glazed look in her eyes.

We stare at each other for a second. She studies Jonah and I wonder if she saw the look we shared. He slips along past us, looking blasé, then vanishes from sight just as quickly.

"I've never seen that guy before," Megan says.

"I met him online."

"What was it like?" She eyes me, suspicious, but I can tell her mind is scrambled.

"F-fun. Just l-like you s-said."

Her look shifts to one of false delight. She hugs me and cries out, "Oh, I'm so happy. Now you're not a virgin any more we really can work together. As equals."

The smell of her skin, her hair, makes me gag. She's rambling and I want her off my case. "I n-need to go to the b-bathroom."

"Do you need a hand? Did you bleed a lot?" she asks, alarmed all of a sudden. "You need to check for tears, make sure you don't end up with an infection."

"It's all okay, th-thanks," I reply and start off down the hall.

She cackles then and shouts after me, "Hey, Alek, was his cock that small? It doesn't count as a proper fuck unless it hurts, you know!"

Her laughter stings all over, my ears, my heart, my skin. I shut the bathroom door and turn the key, then I open the window to get some air. Now I know why there's always so much drink and drugs around. You have to be out of it to survive at this kind of party.

I cry in front of the mirror, upset by what I've seen and heard, by what I had to do tonight, still feeling the hands lunging at me during the strip. I'd like to rinse my face but I don't dare ruin my make-up, so I go back out and gather up my clothes. I pull them on, savouring the feeling of being covered up, safe from prying eyes.

Ruben comes over and grabs my shoulders. He whispers in my ear, "That punter seemed well pleased. I can't wait to try you myself."

I smile at him, turn round and touch him between the legs, a quick but firm gesture. "I can't wait either. B-but that's enough for t-tonight, if y-you don't m-mind."

I lower my eyes.

"Nothing serious?" he asks. "Did the blond guy get carried away? Do you need to go to hospital?"

His concern seems genuine and this throws me.

He said he'd protect me and that's what he's doing, in his own way, in his crazy world. He talks about hospitals as if it was normal, something you'd expect after sex.

"Oh no," I reply. "Everything's fine. I just want to go h-home."

"No problem, you can go just this once," he says, with a sympathetic nod. "But you need to find someone to take you, I can't."

"That's o-okay. Th-thanks."

A few minutes later I'm out in the car with Jonah. He's playing his *Babbling Songs*, the songs that stammer like me, and we let ourselves be carried away by the tunes while our thoughts hang, almost palpable, in the air around us.

I look out the back window and see Ruben's house fading into the distance, getting smaller and smaller. I know that I'll never go back to one of those parties, that I'll never have to sell myself again, whatever the price and whatever the threat. Because I'd rather die than do that one more time.

# 26

"We shouldn't be arguing – we need to make a decision."

"M-maybe tonight isn't the b-best time," I reply, straightening my costume.

Me, Jonah and Helena have shut ourselves in a spare dressing room. It's our first night, there's a lot of excitement in the air and we have two reasons to be worked up.

"You need to go to the police," Jonah repeats, turning to Helena. "It'll be different this time, you'll see. They can do something."

She shakes her head in fury, clenches her fist at Jonah then gives him a kick before barging out, slamming the door behind her.

"She d-doesn't like the p-police," I conclude.

Jonah holds his leg and sits down on a chair that creaks under his weight.

I burst out laughing, but it's more a nervous reaction than anything actually being funny.

"She hates them!" he almost shouts, rubbing his shin. "She hates judges, lawyers, the police. She even hates traffic wardens. Anything that has to do with the law. But she doesn't understand that we're not living in the Wild West, either."

"N-no, she d-doesn't. I've noticed that from the way she handles knives and hammers," I say. "B-but she does have a p-point. Ruben's p-parents are lawyers – powerful, influential people – they'd find a way to bury any charges against him. We need to work out how to really make him pay."

"We don't have time," he reminds me. "When will he want you at another party? Friday? Saturday? You won't be able to keep saying no."

The dressing room door vibrates as someone bangs really loudly on it.

"Five minutes! Jonah to the lights now!"

It's Electra's voice, disappearing down the hall as she shouts more final calls to actors scattered here and there. Despite everything, I love the atmosphere, the anticipation before a performance.

"D-do I look okay?" I ask Jonah, trying to focus on the present.

He stands back up. "You've always been beautiful," he says with a sigh. "In your baggy shirts, in your stage costumes, all the time. When you perform, you're the best."

My whole face burns. I'm not used to compliments from him, from anyone. I almost preferred him when he was sarcastic.

"And now I've seen you with nothing on," he adds

235

playfully, "I have to say you're pretty damn hot like that too."

"S-stop it!" I cry. "That k-kind of talk will get you more k-kicks in the sh-shin."

"I'm only joking, Alek," he whispers. "Break a leg. Go on, knock 'em dead."

"Okay," I say, taking a deep breath.

"A kiss for luck?" he asks.

I blink. But not in confusion. I know what he's asking. I just don't know if I have an answer. He leans in and brushes my lips lightly with his, lingering there for a second as if to breathe me in. I was going to say yes. But he didn't give me time. And now I can taste him on my lips.

My first kiss.

It's like a gentle breeze nudging away the clouds to reveal a new place on the horizon. It tastes good, it tastes honest.

I slap Jonah, right in the face.

"You w-were supposed to w-wait for an answer," I tell him, with a grin.

My heart's pounding and that slap was the only way to release the tension between us. I have to go on stage in five minutes.

"I'll take that as a sign of affection, and a yes," he says, heading over to the door with a hand on the cheek I slapped. "But if you think I'm getting into S&M with you, you've got the wrong guy."

He vanishes down the hall to go and check the lights and sound.

I know he's smiling too; it's a smile that leaves a kind of frisson in its wake.

Only one second but a lot of deep breaths later, I'm on stage, playing Lady Hester. The old theatre is full – Thomas's shows always sell out. I can't see any faces because I'm looking into the light and the audience is in the dark, but I can feel them, the warm anticipation of all those watching us, waiting to be transported to 19th-century England.

"Mr Arbuthnot has a beautiful nature! He is so simple, so sincere. He has one of the most beautiful natures I have ever come across. It is a privilege to meet *him*," I recite, trying to twist towards the wings where Jonah's standing.

I'm thinking of him as I speak, and the line comes from my heart, rather than my diaphragm. I can taste his kiss on my lips and it fills me with happiness and high spirits, just like Lady Hester when she's with Gerald. His kiss illuminates my smile.

It's time for the line I kept messing up in rehearsals. But I attack it. "Nothing should be out of the reach of hope. Life is a hope."

A few moments later, I go off stage.

I head over to Jonah. "Another one please," I say. "It worked a treat."

He kisses me again, a bit deeper this time, for longer.

"Hey, I'm a nice boy, you know," he mumbles before I hurry back on stage.

I've come back from the walk with Gerald and I'm radiant. A few lines later I'm off stage again, my dress swishing and swaying around my legs. It's so nice to be here. It's so nice to be Hester and to be me, all at once.

I go and change my dress – in the second act we're in the Hunstanton Chase drawing room. The roar of applause after the first act reaches me all the way back in my dressing room, and I can't stop myself from smiling. I'm so excited, I drop my hairbrush twice but I manage to tidy myself up and nudge my lopsided wig more or less back into place.

It's time for my monologue.

There'll be no bits of plastic falling from the sky tonight. I just need to let go and summon everything that's been happening inside me during the nine months of rehearsals. Nine months in which I've grown. In which I've learned to listen to my own voice. I sail through the monologue, controlling my syllables, articulating slowly, breathing in and out at the right time. And the finale I give the audience gets a deafening round of applause.

"Oh, your English society seems to me shallow, selfish, foolish ... It has blinded its eyes, and stopped its ears. It lies like a leper in purple. It sits like a dead thing smeared with gold. It is all wrong, all wrong."

There are tears in my eyes. I'm sure that's how Oscar Wilde imagined Lady Hester in this speech. Fragile and indestructible.

In the next passage, I have Ruben in my thoughts.

"A man with a hideous smile and a hideous past. He is asked everywhere. No dinner-party is complete without him. What of those whose ruin is due to him? They are outcasts. They are nameless. If you met them in the street you would turn your head away. I don't complain of their punishment. Let all women who have sinned be punished."

The scene continues and then the second act comes to a close.

We rush away to freshen up and I drink a pint of water then go for a quick wee, making sure my dress doesn't get in the way.

Thomas gives us a clap. "Well done," he says. "You're amazing, all of you."

It dawns on me that this will be our last show together, so I throw my arms round his neck and blurt out, "Th-thanks for everything y-you've done for me over the y-years."

He stares at me and I realise that he knows I've only just understood how important all this is, the Ship of Fools, us, our work together. Only now, when it's all over. He sorts my wig and says, "You'll go far, Aleksandra. You just have to believe in yourself."

The final act is charged with conflicting emotions. Hester has to let go of the harsh way she judges women who've been corrupted, for the good of her beloved Gerald's mother, Mrs Arbuthnot.

The latter walks to the front of the stage and says to her son, "You talk of atonement for a wrong done. What atonement can be made to me? There is no atonement possible. I am disgraced: he is not. That is all. It is the usual history of a man and a woman as it usually happens. And the ending is the ordinary ending. The woman suffers. The man goes free."

Backstage, I bite my nails as I think back to Ruben's words, "No one wants a whore as a girlfriend. Whores are for everyone."

But Jonah stretches over the mixing desk, passing me a tissue and whispering at the same time, "If you cry your make-up will run and you'll be Lady 'Panda Eyes' Hester."

I don't know how he knew I was feeling weepy, given that I had my back to him. But when I turn round, I see that the scene has brought tears to his eyes too. Maybe he understands how I feel.

I go back on stage with my emotions in check and ready to be poured into my final lines.

When Gerald at last says, "Who was it?" and Mrs Arbuthnot replies, "Oh! No one. No one in particular. A man of no importance," we are swept away by the applause.

The final curtain drops and we wait for all the actors, plus Thomas, Helena and Jonah, to join us.

A voice in the audience shouts, "Bravo! Bravo!"

The curtain lifts again and the lights come on, people are on their feet, clapping, and I spot Camilla among them. I scan the first few rows before I remember that my gran didn't come to see me this time and will never be coming again. I'm holding back tears of pain and joy, accepting the embraces of my companions, when I see someone in the front row, just a few metres away.

It's my mum.

She's drying her eyes with a tissue. She shouts, "Amazing, Aleksandra! Aleksandra, you are amazing!" as if she loves my name so much she wants to shout it over and over.

I smile and wave to her, and for a second my world is bright and colourful. Perfect.

Then the audience lets out a collective scream of fear. There's a kind of freak wave, a commotion, the rest of the company starts to panic and Electra shrieks, "Help! A doctor, please! Someone call a doctor!"

I can't work out what's going on.

Until I see Jonah, lying unconscious on the floor.

# 27

As soon as the doctor comes out of Jonah's hospital room, we crowd round her – me, Thomas, Electra and Helena. My mum keeps out the way, but I can feel her there behind me as the doctor explains that Jonah had a mild epileptic fit, that he must have tired himself out over the past few days, maybe because of the show, and that he's susceptible to stress because of his illness.

"Illness?" I find myself asking.

Helena, Thomas and Electra turn to face me. "He's had multiple sclerosis for a few years," Thomas explains with a sigh. "He doesn't like talking about it because he doesn't want people to like him out of pity."

"Why d-did he never t-tell me?" I exclaim, shocked.

"You never asked him," Electra points out, with a look of reproof that I deserve.

I slump in a chair and put my head between my hands.

How could I not have noticed that Jonah was fighting his own battle? For me he was just annoying and childish – Jonah, the theatre hunchback – but I never gave his life any thought, I never asked any questions, not even when I found out he lives in that secret room.

"All he needs is the usual rest and care to get over this fit," the doctor continues. "Are you his next of kin?"

I realise there are no relatives in the room. There's only us – we've never seen his mum and dad.

"Yes," Electra replies firmly. "You can tell us."

Thomas looks at me and Helena, and says, "It's very late. Why don't you go home and get some rest then tomorrow morning, you'll see, Jonah will be back on his feet again."

I don't want to go. I'd rather stay here and try to work it all out. I'd like to stay close to Jonah. But Helena makes for the door so I nod and follow her silently, signalling to my mum on the way out. Helena starts kicking stones in the car park, and I realise how angry she is. We ask if she wants a lift but she shakes her head and goes off on her own, almost running.

My mum drives home in silence while I mull it over, looking out at the quiet, sleeping city sliding past. I glance over at her every now and then, and all I see in her features is someone I don't know. I wonder how you can live with people without ever really knowing them. Jonah's words come back to mind – "The only one wrapped up in herself here is you."

It must be true. I don't notice what's happening to the people around me.

When we get home, I pull out my mum's blue diary. I'd put it in a drawer the day she gave it to me.

I read it from the start, trying to focus on every word, every nuance hidden between the lines. It hurts but I need to do it. I have the feeling that if I want to be listened to, I need to start listening too. So I relive my life through my mum's eyes. I put her centre stage and find out that I was always indifferent to her when she saw me and this stopped her from taking me back to live with her. My habit of keeping everything in, my fear of showing my feelings and of being rejected, were interpreted differently from the outside. It hurt my mum. It kept us apart. It's still separating us now.

By the time I finish reading and working my way through all the photos, it's three in the morning. I'd spent hours crying, laughing, seeing my life through different eyes. I'd forced myself to look properly at the photo of my dad.

I get up and go into the hall.

When I get to my mum's bedroom, I open the door.

"Mum?" I call out quietly. The word sounds different now. She rolls over in bed and replies, "Hmmm? Matt?"

"No, it's Aleksandra," I whisper. "Can you come here for a second, please?"

She springs up, as if getting up in the middle of the night for me were normal, and this reassures me. Her pyjama-clad silhouette moves through the shadows. We leave her room and go into the living room.

"I j-just wanted a hug, but I've n-never dared ask," I begin, lowering my eyes. I've always waited for her to come to me, but I never opened my arms to welcome her.

She doesn't say anything, just takes a few steps forwards and squeezes me.

She squeezes me so hard, it's like all the hugs we've never had, all at once, and I can smell her smell, similar to mine, and I feel like a child again, for a few precious seconds. We stay like that. I let her stroke my hair and listen to my name as she says it over and over, in a quiet voice. We pull apart, our hearts overflowing, and she makes two herbal teas, telling me that we've got all the time in the world. No one will ever come between us again.

I see Ruben's sneering face waiting for me. What will my mum think of me when she finds out what I did? Holding my cup in my hand, letting its warmth give me strength, I say, "G-Gran never had a g-good word to say about y-you. She used to s-say that you'd b-been easy with b-boys and that's why you let the f-first one you m-met get y-you p-pregnant."

She gives a sad smile. "She never forgave me for falling for the wrong boy."

"I know," I reply.

Then she sighs. "But my dad walked out on your gran when she had three young children to bring up, she had no money, no home. After that, she never thought much of men – all men."

I nod. I know the story. Gran wanted my future to be different from the pasts of the other Ramelli women. And instead fate seems to have dealt us a cruel blow; we've all been condemned to fall for the wrong guy.

"My relationship with Hadrijan was actually a

wonderful, loving thing," my mum continues. "I was terrified, but having you is something I'd never change, even if I could turn the clock back."

It's a nice thing to hear her say – it sounds true, and I savour it because I need her words to bolster my spirits.

"I h-have to tell you s-something," I mumble.

"I'm listening," my mum replies, just like Jonah.

I take a breath and tell her my story.


I don't leave anything out, not even when I glimpse something verging on horror in her eyes, then anger, then helplessness.

I'm stuttering a lot. The syllables get mixed up in the flood of tears I'm determined to hold in. But I tell it all. I explain about Jonah and the video we made, the £3,000 I'd saved in the suitcase under my bed, and then how I'd used it to stop Ruben selling my first time to a stranger.

She sighs and shuts her eyes.

"How could I not have noticed?" she keeps repeating.

"He's clever," I say to reassure her. "You d-don't see his t-true face until it's t-too late. And I l-lied to y-you."

She looks at me. "He makes young girls fall in love with him then he sells them. And I welcomed him into our home. I let Matt sit on his knee," she says, almost to herself. Her voice is shaking.

"The f-fact is I n-never said n-no to him," I confess. "He always a-asked if I w-wanted to. And I always w-went along with whatever he w-wanted, thinking he'd like me m-more. I was s-stupid."

My mum puts a hand on my arm. "Look at me, Alek," she says in a tough voice. "Ruben is forcing young girls into prostitution. He gave you drugs. He sold you. There are laws that can stop him. The naivety of the girls he exploits can't justify what he does."

I explain Helena's fear of authority. I tell her how powerful Ruben's parents are and how they would destroy me.

I even manage to tell her that Ruben is blackmailing me with a video. Then Luke appears in the room, his hair tousled and his face confused.

"What's going on?" he asks, alarmed.

My mum looks at me, as if to ask my permission to tell him.

What I want is to say, "I'm ashamed."

And that's what I do say. "I'm s-so ashamed of m-myself."

It is such a relief to get it out. Then I add, "But I can't hide what I did. Maybe Luke'll know how to help me."

But Luke goes off his head when he hears the truth about what's been happening right under his nose these past few months. He can't believe Ruben tricked him in his own house. He leaps to his feet, runs a hand through his hair then grabs the car keys, saying, "I'm going to teach him a lesson." Then he stops, exclaiming, "No, I've got a better idea." His face lights up as he turns to my mum. "Run a feature on it – for your network!"

We both stare, mouths gaping. We hadn't thought of television, how it's still the fastest, safest way to spread a news story so no one can pretend it doesn't exist.

I see elation spark in my mum's eyes. "You're right. I can destroy him. The police will be forced to investigate."

Animated, as if they've found the answer, they go over all the details, but I start to wonder. What will happen after? Megan and Ruben's threats fly around in my head, buzzing spitefully. I wish I could just go away somewhere, start all over, forget what I was, what I did.

Mum sees I'm not sure and comes to sit beside me on the sofa.

"Tell us what you think, Aleksandra," she says. "Could you handle a court case?"

I don't want anyone to see Ruben's video. That girl who's worse than me has the same face, the same body, the same eyes as me. No one will believe me if she's there in front of us. No one will believe a whore. I'm scared. And I tell them that.

"I'm not going to say it'll be easy, because it won't be," my mum replies solemnly. "They'll accuse you of all sorts, they'll call you all kinds of horrible names. It's not a world away from what happened to me seventeen years ago, and going abroad didn't help me to forget or to right the wrongs."

"It's your decision," Luke says. He has a kind look on his face, as if he'd like to come over and hug me but doesn't want to intrude on the mother–daughter closeness. "We'll be with you whatever you decide."

"We will," my mum agrees. "But it's late, you're shattered. Why don't you sleep on it?"

But sleeping is impossible.

I stare up at the ceiling as if it were a giant screen on which to project my thoughts. I'm alone but I'm not alone. Some people will stay by my side; others will try to ruin me. Most people will judge me and condemn me. Just like it says in the play, women will suffer, and men will go free. Or perhaps not. I think about ways that I can change things. I think about being fragile and indestructible. I think about Jonah and how he expects me to be strong enough to save those girls who could end up like me. I wonder if those girls will want to be saved or if they would rather be like Megan, part of her darkly glittering world.

I think about Jonah in hospital, his secret illness, his strength and his energy. I think about Helena's furious hammer, all that anger bubbling away inside her like a pot about to boil over, and the fact that she expects me to act, to do something.

And I see the video again; it reels through my mind, every image stamped into my brain.

The people around me, would they really still love me if they saw it? Will I still be the same person in their eyes? Will anyone bother to think about the person – the girl with feelings, fears and emotions – hiding behind that whore?

My heart aches.

My vision clouds over.

What should I do?

What should I do?

# 28

Jonah takes up the whole sofa; he's too tall and he needs to lie down.

So the rest of us perch on chairs and on the little two-seater sofa in front of the television, which is switched on. It's been a few days now and we had to act quickly otherwise Ruben would have been suspicious. While my mum has been putting together her special report in the production room, I've been hanging out at the shopping centre with Megan and the others, pretending everything's fine.

It hasn't been easy for Mum; the strain is showing on her face.

She's spent night after night in front of the computer, looking grey the morning after. "I recognised the daughter of a woman from work," she told me. "She's twelve. Just twelve years old."

I looked at her and felt hot guilt coursing through me. She wouldn't be mixed up in this story if I'd looked after myself. One night I heard her arguing with Luke and I couldn't stop myself from creeping along the hall to their bedroom, to eavesdrop. I was scared stiff that she'd want to send me away, that she'd finally realise just how much trouble I had willingly got myself into.

But what I heard her say was, "I treated her like an adult. I've always treated her like an adult, ever since she was born. What on earth was I thinking? What on earth?"

I heard her voice break into sobs, then Luke saying, "Lara, love, you shouldn't blame yourself."

"Oh yes I should. It's my fault. I should've protected her and I didn't. She said she wanted a hug and I didn't give her one. What kind of a mother am I?"

Luke shushed her; he wouldn't let her drag up the past. "Focus on now, on the future," he said. "We all have to move on; sorting this thing out will help bring you closer."

I went back to bed, aware that the burning shame I feel inside, now the fear has subsided, will take a long, long time to go away. Maybe it never will, maybe I'll just have to learn to live with it.

Now that I'm here, though, surrounded by my family – that's what we are, after all – and my friends, waiting for my mum's report to air, I'm terrified.

We don't know what to expect.

We don't know how our town will react.

Helena's sitting on the floor in front of Jonah, shaking her head constantly, as if she disapproves of the whole idea. She's still convinced we should have done something much tougher, more brutal, like paying someone to beat Ruben to a pulp. At least that's what she told Jonah in one of her messages, saying that at least there's a chance of justice in the Wild West.

I don't know who's right. I don't know if any of us are right. I'm here with everyone else, watching, no idea what to expect. I didn't want to see the report before it was broadcast.

When the theme tune starts to play, no one utters a word. To be honest, no one dares to breathe. The titles flash up.

"What dark secrets lurk behind the night-life of small towns? Lara Ramelli reveals the shocking reality in an exclusive investigative report on the private parties where sex takes centre stage."

"With an opening like that, we should get everyone's attention," my mum remarks under her breath.

Then the footage starts to roll with shots showing Jonah's point of view. Luckily he's tall, so the camera angle from the breast pocket of his jacket was just right and the video he took at Ruben's beach house came out perfectly.

I spot Ruben straight away; he's easily recognisable despite the post-production blur put over his face to protect his identity.

"I'm here for the virgin," Jonah says, shaking Ruben's hand. "But how do I know it's her first time? You can never be sure with these girls nowadays."

He sounds coarse and unpleasant; he must have picked up his acting skills from hanging around the theatre all this time. I'm shaking like a leaf. I was head over heels in love with the young man on screen, but now he looks like a complete stranger.

"Oh she's a virgin all right," Ruben replies, obligingly. "I prepared her personally. It took a while but she's ready now, she knows exactly what's expected of her."

He's talking about me. I can feel the tears welling up.

"Anyway, with those tits, it'll be like all your porno fantasies come true," he adds, indicating me.

Jonah looks over at me too and asks, "Can I do what I want?"

The two of them snigger, like old mates, then Ruben says, "Yeah, course, but no violence, our girls are important to us. Anything else goes. Have your fun. She'll do anything you say."

Money changes hands then the two of them come over to me, the camera now pointing straight at me. The girls' private parts have been blurred, but you can still see we're naked.

"Come and sit here," Luke says, moving over to let me in between him and my mum on the two-seater sofa.

I am rigid with nerves, but I go over and sink into their embrace.

"He is such a worthless human being," Luke whispers, "he's not even worth punching."

I try to smile, even though I feel like the worthless one. Then we watch as the camera pans round the house with the party in full swing. Jonah was very conscientious, I think. He filmed each room, and in every one people are having sex, in one way or another. Including the hall and

253

the living room, where all the girls are busy with someone now that the strip's over. Jonah goes over to the drinks table and picks up a beer. He turns to a guy standing next to him and asks, "You come here often?"

"Yeah," the guy says, clinking his bottle against Jonah's. "Ruben's parties are the best. Who'd you fuck?"

"A virgin," Jonah replies, steady as anything.

I can't quite believe how he managed to stay in control and blend in so well with them.

"You're minted, mate," the other one says. "I'd kill for a young one, maybe twelve or thirteen. How old was yours?"

"Sixteen, but her tits were worth what I paid for her."

They laugh and clink bottles again.

Then I hear the narrator's voice, my mum's voice, as she comments on each scene.

We watch the alcohol flowing, and the drugs. We hear Jonah ask Ruben, "You got one of those pills for me too?"

"Sorry, mate – I don't deal," Ruben says. "I only use them with the girls, to loosen them up a bit, you know. But I can give you my dealer's number."

Helena's banging her foot hard on the floor. Then she jumps up and starts pacing round the room. We don't stop her; we just hope she won't break anything.

In the final scene, Jonah goes over to Ruben to say goodbye.

"Here's my number. You want a girl, you know where to find me."

Jonah takes the card Ruben's holding out to him.

It's framed on the screen with the details pixelated out.

"Definitely. But I need to know what I'm getting," Jonah says, his face turning hard. "This lot are just kids. I like a dirty fuck, you know, proper anal, stuff like that. Can you get me that?"

"No problem," Ruben says, his smile as confident as ever. "Whatever you want. As long as you've got the money."

They laugh.

Then Ruben says, "Hey, mate, tell me one thing."

It looks as if Jonah's fiddling with the camera. I guess he's making some kind of gesture we can't see.

"How was it?" Ruben asks. "Was she any good? I've spent a lot of money on her, so I'd appreciate hearing from the man who broke her in."

"I wouldn't have taken your number if she hadn't been worth what you charged for her."

I look at Jonah. He looks at me. He couldn't keep the act up in the end; he couldn't talk about me as if we'd actually had sex.

"This is when I really wanted to make him suffer," he says out loud and I realise how worn out he must be too, and not only by his condition.

The scene switches to my mum in the studio.

She's speaking to a panel of experts, talking about grooming and the sexual exploitation of children and how society should best deal with it.

Some experts blame the media, the over-sexualisation of children in TV programmes, advertising and music videos. Some blame drugs and alcohol. And some blame online porn. Others talk about our consumer society in which sex has become a commodity to be bought and sold just like any other.

They don't have any answers.

Just empty words from a group of adults who've never been naked, dancing for money in front of a baying crowd.

When the report finishes, my mum gets up and picks up the phone.

"Brace yourselves," she announces, as it rings seconds later.

It's like all hell has broken loose. Most calls are from people wanting to spit venom at my mum, telling her she should be ashamed of herself for airing her dirty laundry in public like that, that she should mind her own business instead of ruining the lives of innocent families.

We knew that a lot of people would recognise sons, daughters, grandchildren, relatives and friends. It terrifies me that their first instinct on seeing the town's young girls being sold for sex is to shoot the messenger.

They're all against us. No one rings for an explanation or to ask for help or to support us.

Each time the phone rings, my mum shouts into it, slams it down and it rings again. We can hear the frantic, constant beep of message alerts too.

"Keep calm," she says, practically screaming at us. "This happens when you're a journalist. They take it out on you as if it's your fault. God only knows what's happening online."

She keeps picking up the phone until she unplugs the whole unit and hurls it at the wall, smashing it to smithereens.

Helena claps her hands. The rest of us gawp; we're shattered too.

The bell rings a few seconds later and Luke goes to open the door. It's some people they know, parents of girls I've seen at the parties, and they're screaming at him, demanding to know that their kids' lives aren't like what they've just seen on TV.

They want to negotiate the truth, and refuse to listen when my mum says it's not her they should be attacking.

"Aleksandra, why don't you and your friends go to your room," Luke suggests.

We comply, overwhelmed by how the adults are reacting. No one wants to protect us girls. They want to accuse us instead.

Helena leads the way but she turns round to shake her fist at everyone, and I know it means, "I told you so."

"Oh J-Jonah," I sigh, sitting down on the bed. "Have we made a huge mistake?"

"We need to wait," he says. "This is just an emotional, knee-jerk reaction. The police will decide what happens next."

Helena laughs. She plants her hands on her hips, glares at us and then storms out the room, leaving us alone. We hear the front door bang.

"It's like when you're sick, isn't it?" Jonah tries to lighten the mood. "First there's the acute stage, then the intensive treatment, then you start to heal."

"Or you die," I retort.

"Or you die. Right."

He lies down on the bed and I can't help but snuggle in beside him. He holds me tight and together we listen to the shouts coming from the lounge.

"I wish they'd just go to hell," Jonah says after a bit, but then he starts to sing one of his songs. He's got a lovely voice. It fills up the room and drowns out the yelling.

*Tomorrow will be tomorrow*
*People always forget*
*Even if they break the silence*
*People always forget*

He sings until I fall asleep, never letting me go.

# 29

When I saw the court from the car, I felt like turning back.

It's a big square building, all washed-out and sad; it definitely doesn't stir the reassuring sense of justice I was expecting. It could be a hospital or a prison, or even the entrance to a graveyard.

But I followed my mum and Luke in. I took Jonah's hand when he held it out to me from the main entrance where he was waiting, dressed in a suit and tie, and now I'm outside the court room waiting to be called as a witness.

I'm alone.

A long grey corridor stretches out to my right and left, with wooden benches lining the walls and a few faded pictures hanging here and there, failing to brighten the place up.

It's just me and my family.

The only person who agreed to testify against Ruben was Jonah.

Ruben's parents will destroy Jonah; he's got no family, no home, and is squatting in the theatre.

They twisted his life around to make him look like

some sort of radical misfit even though it's not his fault his alcoholic mum and violent dad kicked him out a few years ago, forcing him to fend for himself. No one cares about his music, or him going out on a limb to help me, or how he's worked honestly for Thomas and the Ship of Fools for the past three years.

I'd like to be able to turn back the clock. I'd like to run away from this case, this court, but I can see how committed my mum, Luke and Jonah are – it wouldn't be right for me to chicken out now. I've decided to go all the way, and this time I'll have to accept the consequences.

While I sit biting my nails, I hear the tip-tap of heels coming from the main entrance. The sound echoes along the empty hall, coming closer until a figure appears round the corner, wiggling its way towards me until it finally comes into focus.

It's a tall, slim blonde. She's wearing a blue suit with a knee-length skirt and high heels. She's carrying a quirky, asymmetrical bag and on her impish face I see a swollen black eye, like that of a boxer who's taken a knock-out right hand.

I can't believe my eyes. I get up from the bench, intending to go and fetch my mum. I'm sure she's here to get even, to take revenge, just like she promised, but she's not really looking at me at all and just flops onto the bench beside me with a tired sigh.

"Take it easy," she says, crossing her arms in front of her. "My mum's parking the car. I'm here to testify against those pricks."

She starts to cry and I notice how tears trickle from her swollen eye too.

"See what he's done to me?" she asks, pulling a sad smile. "He was a shit boyfriend."

She's talking about Lee. She raises her hand to show me the ring she's still wearing.

"I even had to buy this myself," she confesses.

I'm speechless. I didn't expect her to come, not today. None of the girls agreed to be witnesses; they didn't want to be caught up in it all and be forced to admit they were part of the ring too. After all, I'm the one who pressed charges. They all denied it. They said I sold sex at the parties because I needed the money for drugs and that they kept telling me to ask someone for help.

People believed them, especially since most of the girls involved are from good families. Why on earth would they behave in such a degrading way?

I, on the other hand, have got a record as long as my arm with social services. This is just another stigma that will be hard for me to shake off, branding me in the eyes of the judge.

"Do you want a laugh?" Megan continues. "For the first time in my life, my mum's actually on my side. Crazy, huh?"

I nod, unsure. I still don't know what to think. She told a pack of lies about me and our friendship to the reporters. Lying comes easy to her; she could even be lying now, hiding behind her black eye.

"Lee punched me when he got the court summons,"

she tells me. "He said it was my fault, that I was the one who brought you in and ruined everything. He beat me up so bad I thought I was going to die."

"I d-didn't know he h-hit you," I venture. I remember the slap I caught sight of at one of the first parties and the bruises she had every now and then, but she always made light of them, spinning us stories and defending him.

"He was a shit boyfriend," she says again, slumping back, as if she'd like to disappear. She looks a lot less sure of herself than she normally does. "I want him put behind bars. And I hope they seize all the money he creamed off me in the past three years."

I realise that Lee is Megan's Ruben. I see that now. I sit down beside her and sigh. It all seems too big, this terrible thing, and us so small in the face of it. How will we ever manage to bear such a load? Where will we start over from?

Megan rummages around in her bag and hands me a bulging envelope.

"This is yours," she says. "I know we'll never be proper friends, but I wanted to apologise somehow."

I open the envelope, expecting to find money inside that I'll refuse, but instead there's a phone. I look at her questioningly. The hint of a cheeky smile flickers across her face.

"It's Ruben's," she says. "I nicked it off him a few nights ago. It's got the video of you, and films he made of the other girls too." She shrugs. "No doubt he's got a copy of it somewhere, but at least we got this off him. It's a start."

"Thanks," I say, surprised. It means a lot that she did this for me. I know how risky it must've been for her. She thought of me when she could've chosen not to. "We'll m-make him p-pay. T-together," I add.

"Oh, I don't know about that," she says, flippant again. "Do you know what Ruben's parents have done? They've bought him a motorbike. To show people they're not punishing him, that they support him and believe his version of events."

His version.

His lawyer parents issued a statement to say he never asked girls to strip, or to have any kind of sexual activity with anyone. No one can accuse him of grooming or sexual abuse, they say. His parties were just young people having a bit of fun, until a maladjusted teenage girl came along. They claim I was after some easy money and was willing to drag our community through the mud for my own personal gain.

In their opinion, my mum's report proves nothing. They're disparaging her and her profession, trying to convince people it's a slanderous hoax. Everyone knows that I'm her daughter and the people of our town will just believe what they want to.

I understand them.

Who would put their own peace and safety at risk to save girls like us?

But if the rules of this world are wrong, maybe it's only right that we're trying to change them to make sense of what happened to us, just like Jonah said.

Which is why, when the door to the court room opens and the usher nods at me to enter, I wish Megan good luck and stride forward, ready to tell the truth.

The whole truth, and nothing but the truth.

# 30

"You can't catch me!"

Megan pedals in the summer sun, oblivious to the heat.

I can see the back of her blue top and her pale legs going round and round, following the motion of the wheels. I try to keep up but the sun is making me sweat. The breeze I'm whipping up makes me smile, though, so I pedal harder.

School's out.

The court case is just beginning.

The only way to survive is to keep moving, like we're doing now, pushing on the pedals so we don't fall off, don't stop and burn in the pitiless sun.

We cycle across the city, shades of painted concrete flashing past but failing to touch us; we're faster. We pass the sad supermarkets, car parks baking in the stifling heat, lines of cars sizzling like the white-hot water of a river, a hostage to its own banks. It's all so vivid and so remote. So near, but immaterial. If I were to reach out, I probably wouldn't feel anything; these are just the false images of a world that doesn't exist for me.

What's real is Megan's blue top, her blonde ponytail, her flip-flops on the pedals. Jonah's hand is real, the one that squeezes mine every time he sees shadows flit across my eyes, making me think I must be sending out telepathic messages. My mum's hug, every night before I go to bed, is real. And my new family, which includes a brother whose every second word is *why*, and a stepdad who didn't judge me.

We reach the suburbs and in the distance I can see the shopping centre where Megan used to go with the girls. Megan, whose name isn't actually Megan. She made me swear never to tell anyone her real name, because she's embarrassed by it. It was her grandmother's name. My gran's name, on the other hand, has slipped back into the shadows, and isn't quite as painful. Because life goes on, and we need to understand and get through the time we have left, as best we can.

"Are y-you sure w-we're going the r-right way?" I shout.

"No. I'm just following my instincts," she replies, and then laughs.

At night she cries her heart out; in the daytime she cries with the therapist she's been seeing. Her mum insisted she talk to someone and I think it's helping. She has more wounds than me to heal, and she's been sewing mountains of clothes. She has created almost an entire collection already and her mum no longer denies her the money she needs for material.

Carla's trying to accept her daughter as different from her.

"There it is! I see the red bricks."

Not too far away, we spy an open space in the shade
of a stand of trees, and among them an old, disused
building. There, sitting on some kind of wheelbarrow that
looks a bit like a moped, is Jonah. His long golden hair
is glinting in the sun, peeping out at the side of his face
from his red bandana. He smiles and waves with his free
arm, keeping the other one behind his back.

He waits for us to get off our bikes then brings his
other arm round, holding it out in front of us. In his
hand is a kids' water pistol, fully loaded, which he starts
squirting before we've had time to realise what's hit us.

Megan and I scream and start running across the
dusty yard, but he's right behind us and I can hear him
laughing even if I can't see him for the water in my eyes.
I feel his arms round me, a kiss on my forehead. I try to
blink.

"My h-hair will go all f-frizzy," I say, dripping water.

"My heart goes all frizzy when I see you," he whispers
in my ear.

"Hey, lovebirds, I'm here too if you hadn't noticed,"
Megan says, hands on hips.

Jonah sighs and lets me go, then sprays the rest of the
water on his neck to cool down. He still doesn't know
how to take Megan. He realises she was a victim like me,
but he can't forgive her for throwing me into Ruben's
clutches – and from there to the wolves.

I asked him to try and forgive her, as I am. There's a
huge sadness in her big bright eyes, as if she'd woken up

from a nightmare and found that real life is actually ten times worse. She's like a caged animal at times, frantic and distraught; that's when I see the light in her bedroom window and know she's in there, sewing, sketching, cutting, creating, trying to find peace.

"Helena's late," she points out, looking at her watch.

"Are y-you s-sure we can g-go in?" I ask Jonah. The red-brick building looks asleep with its boarded-up windows.

He shrugs. "We'll stay as long as we can. The council doesn't need it any more – maybe we can convince them to let us use it."

A low droning reaches us, like a large insect getting closer. We peer into the distance until we see Helena on her moped. Her only concession to the summer heat is that she's now wearing short dungarees. The combat boots are still on her feet and the tool belt round her waist.

She bounces over with a spring in her step and light in her eyes.

She bows in greeting.

"What have you been up to?" Jonah asks, suspicious.

She shrugs and smiles. Then she points to the house, as if to say, "Are we going in or not?"

We go in.

Jonah's been here for a few days giving it a basic clean, and he brought out his stuff from the theatre, because he couldn't stay there any more. The boxes full of props, costumes and various objects that Thomas gave us are sitting in a corner.

We throw the windows wide open and let the sunlight flood into the main room, a spacious warehouse at the front of the building.

We sit round an old table, looking at each other, hesitant.

"I've got some figures," Jonah starts, spreading out sheets of paper in front of him. "If Helena deals with scenery, Megan with costumes and Aleksandra with directing and auditions, we're half way there. What we're missing is money for materials and to smarten this place up a bit."

"We c-can get the odd j-job here and th-there," I suggest. "In the s-summer."

"Definitely," he agrees. "But it won't be enough."

"What about selling your music?" Megan suggests.

Jonah raises an eyebrow and says, "Even if I could, I'd have to go on tour and what would you guys do without me?"

There's no answer to that and we giggle.

"My m-mum will h-help out," I add. "M-maybe we c-could find a s-sponsor."

It doesn't sound very likely. Who'd want to sponsor four outcasts trying to put together a musical written by someone who's little more than a vagrant?

"You could've said you were after a sponsor," Megan says, looking serious. "That's not a problem."

"Do you know s-someone?" I ask, cheering up.

"Oh, yes. She's sitting right in front of you."

Jonah points at her. "You?"

"Yes, me. I've decided to invest my money in us," she says. "You think it sounds crazy? My therapist says it will help me."

No one says a word.

We've never talked about that money.

But Megan's pulling an envelope out of her bag and holding out a wad of banknotes. "Here's a grand, for starters, to get the paint and stuff."

"Th-thanks so much!" I whoop, clapping my hands. Helena and Jonah look on. "Well? What's up with you two? It's amazing, w-we can s-start right away."

"Where did you get it?" Jonah asks.

"You know the answer to that full well," she says, waving her hand in annoyance. "There's more than ten grand here. I don't want a penny of it, but I can't exactly throw it away either. My mum suggested I give it to charity, so I tried to think of someone who needed charity, and right now that would be us. Do you have anything against that?"

Jonah looks at her with a hint of a smile. "No. It makes perfect sense. What do you think, Helena?"

Helena nods, squirming on her chair, still beaming.

"Good. That's settled. And now at least we'll have something to do until the next hearing and I won't go stir crazy," Megan adds with a sigh.

She's right. We're trying to ignore it but we all know it's going to take a while.

Journalists from all over keep running reports on our story, interviewing some of the older girls who are willing to tell a few lies to take the heat off themselves and paint us in a bad light.

The first few weeks after the trial began were hellish. We had reporters lying in wait in the garden with their cameras. They offered me money for an exclusive interview, but I turned them down. I don't want to become a sensation. I just want justice and to get on with my life as best I can.

But the reporters refuse to back down, digging around in our lives and phoning us constantly despite the media blackout my mum requested.

The only good news from the investigation is that the police have seized and blocked all Ruben's videos, which means the images of that worse-than-me girl will never make it out into the world now.

The hardest thing for us to take is that Lee and Ruben are out on bail and their lives haven't been affected at all, for the time being at least. We occasionally see them around town on their motorbikes. The girl called Tess on the intercom turned out to be not Ruben's sister but his official girlfriend, who went on television to make a personal appeal to me.

Looking straight into the camera and moving her immaculately lipsticked mouth, she said, "You can't ruin the life of a bright young man like Ruben out of vengeance for your own misfortunes. You know in your heart that the only guilty one here is you."

Helena texted me afterwards. "Birdbrain can't even speak properly. Vengeance for your own misfortunes is the most Neanderthal thing I've ever heard."

But then, all of a sudden, a black cloud seems to descend over the red-brick warehouse.

Helena takes off her tool belt and bangs it on the table, with such force that it almost bounces off the hard surface.

"I knew it," Jonah groans.

She ignores him and pulls out her tools, one by one, lining them up as if to make a display of them for us.

She finishes off by digging down into her pocket and pulling out a small metal object that she places in front of us, beside her tools.

"You really did it," Jonah says.

"Listen, I might not have the best mental health in the world, but you lot, you're really not in a good place," Megan comments, at a loss to understand what's going on.

I look at the object, a piece of metal with writing engraved on it. It's a crest, the kind you see on the body of motorbikes.

"What's th-this?" I ask, confused.

Jonah throws his hands up in the air. "Don't look at me for an explanation!" he cries. "I don't want to get drawn into this. I said that from the start."

Helena kicks him under the table but he doesn't dodge it, rubbing his shin instead and refusing to back down.

"Okay, l-let's try and g-guess," I say. "Did you b-buy a motorbike?"

She picks up the hammer and bangs it on the table.

Megan squeals and shakes her head.

"Where d-did you g-get this c-crest?" I ask, nervous now.

Helena punches her right fist into her left palm and looks me in the eye. She's deadly serious and not smiling.

"From R-Ruben's motorbike?"

She nods. Her eyes are twinkling now.

"She didn't just take the crest, if you must know," Jonah explodes, unable to keep quiet any longer. "She dismantled his whole bike, bit by bit. And I mean everything, down to the nuts and bolts. She was in his garage last night. Do you get it now? Go on, say something to her. Tell her she'll get locked up sooner or later."

Helena makes a victory sign.

Megan starts laughing. "I don't believe it. How on earth did you do that?"

I want to laugh too, I can't hold it in. It doesn't solve anything, but the picture of Ruben's face as he goes into the garage, all dressed up in his hip biker clothes, only to find his precious baby laid out like a kids' model kit on the floor, well, it does relieve the tension a bit.

"There's nothing to laugh about," Jonah says, appalled. "It's a crazy act by a crazy person."

"Oh, that's where you're wrong," Megan hits back, still in hysterics. "I'll be laughing for the next six months. Thanks, sweetie."

Helena nods and starts laughing too.

"I'm not sure I want to work with three women after all," Jonah says, folding his arms over his chest and watching us as we double over laughing.

We all get up and surround him, as coordinated as if we'd agreed it beforehand, then the three of us tickle him until he gives in and starts laughing and shouting "I SURRENDER" as he falls off his chair. We all fall on top of him and I worry that he might get hurt or have another fit, but when I look at him he winks and my world lights up again. You and me, we'll take things one step at a time, I think.

Like cleaning this place and turning it into a theatre.

That's our next task.

We take a brush and a cloth each. We fill buckets with water. Jonah puts on his music. The notes are loud and clear, summer is marching on, and we're here, fragile and indestructible, united by a past that, as weird and difficult as it may be, is ours.

"Okay, g-guys, let's g-get started," I yell. "We'll s-sort it all out, one w-way or another."

And I know we will. I really believe it.

# Epilogue

We could do with a happy ending, I think, as the room starts filling up and Jonah argues with the police outside. The two officers are frowning and shaking their heads. Once. Then again. But then one smiles. His forehead smoothes and his face relaxes. Jonah must be working his magic again. By the time I look back, the two officers are inside the main hall, surveying the room. In the end, they lean against the back wall and look like they're staying, almost like they're waiting for the show to start, with the rest of the audience.

I put Matt down, getting him off my knee where he's been parked since he came in, and send him back to my mum and Luke in the front row. A front row of folding chairs.

I go into the makeshift wings beside the makeshift stage in this cobbled-together theatre that has been part of my wonky life for the past few months. Megan has pins in her mouth and her eyes are wide. She's putting the finishing touches to the costumes, just five minutes before the actors go on stage. Her mum's in the front row beside mine, gripping a pack of tissues in her hands, ready to stem the flood of tears she's expecting.

The fact is, stories never really end, there's just a series of transitions, doors opening and closing, and these wings leading into the action.

Helena pushes the scenery for the first act into place and we're all set. I know this because she tells me.

"Okay," she says.

It's the one word she's been saying for a while now, and it bodes well for the future. One little word with a big message.

"Are we ready? I promised those cops the best show they've ever seen," Jonah cries, out of breath. "But I reckon they're just hanging around to arrest me afterwards."

I look at him and laugh. He had another attack a few weeks ago because of the stress of the musical, but he got over it and his big mouth doesn't seem to be any the worse for it. Or his kisses. It's not true that no one wants a whore. Maybe it's the wrong word; after all, what does it really mean? Megan says that labels are for people with no imagination. The way you are inside, the way the world sees you, the way you'd like the world to see you, are complex truths hanging together in a shaky alliance.

I look in the mirror every now and then and wonder, *Who are you*? I asked Jonah once too. "What do you think – who am I really?"

"The girl I love," he replied. "That aside, you need to find your own answer. But I don't think that'll happen for at least another ninety-five years."

He's right.

If you think about it, we're like prisms. We might give ourselves a shape because we find boundaries reassuring, but we're constantly changing, from fragile and uncertain to self-assured and indestructible, dead and re-born a thousand times over.

"It's your turn," Megan whispers, shoving me out onto the stage. The shower of applause engulfs me like warm summer rain.

I breathe in. I breathe out.

I am Aleksandra. With a 'k' in the middle.

And that's all I need.

# Acknowledgements

This page at the end of books is never original. All writers seem to have lovely partners who support them along the way, and family and friends who encourage them. I am no exception. Without my husband Marco, my mum Ada and my dad Annibale, my brother Giorgio and sister-in-law Silvia, my creative journey would have been much more difficult and lonely. My friends – too many to be named here – have always been by my side, bearing patiently my overwhelming enthusiasms and my dark moments.

But it's thanks to still more people that you can read *Girl Detached* today.

All my teachers, from Bridget Ross at the British Council in Rome, to Lisa Sainsbury, David Rudd and Ariel Kahn at Roehampton University – they all have been, and some still are, invaluable mentors. They never saw a stranger in me, just a children's writer trying to find a new way to be heard.

Denise Muir, my translator, and Marinella Mezzanotte, my personal copyeditor – without them I would be lost in translation. Our discussions about the use of a single word can go back and forth for dozens of emails; for that reason I love them both.

Lastly, I would like to thank all gatekeepers, Italian ones in particular. Thanks to them I have learned that I am a controversial author. I used to think I was just a plain, ordinary children's writer, but they gave me a fabulous new identity, one which has brought me here. Where? To the Bucket List! And, yes, I really want to thank its wonderful crew for their commitment, their friendliness, and for their brave mission to give space and voice to diversity in every possible way. *Grazie.*

## About Manuela Salvi

Manuela Salvi is the author of over 20 books for children and young people in her native Italy. She is inspired by controversial themes and loves to give her characters a chance to be brave and to challenge and change the world around them. But, after the original version of *Girl Detached* was banned by Italian censors, Manuela moved to London, where she is studying for a PhD at the University of Roehampton. Manuela says that she is "now writing about mooning guerrillas, outcasts and drag queens" and that when she's not writing, she finds herself spending "a fortune on tons of books that she will never have enough time to read".